DEATH
D ● T

First published in Great Britain
in 2016

ISBN

978 1 5272 0451 5

This book is a work of fiction and any resemblance to actual persons,
living or dead, is purely coincidental.

DEATH
D●T

QUANTALORE

For James

The conclusion, therefore, is that multiple worlds automatically occur in quantum mechanics. They are an inevitable part of the formalism. The only remaining question is: what are you going to do about it? There are three popular strategies on the market: anger, denial, and acceptance.

Sean Carroll, *Cosmologist*
Why the Many-Worlds Formulation of Quantum Mechanics Is Probably Correct
(2014)

Chapter One

Pranks

The ratchety squawk of gulls taken to rooftops and telephone poles intensified as high tide rolled in. Their calls to debris washing ashore echoed off the craggy steeps surrounding Trebullan. As we sat on the clifftops, listening to boats bob along the two piers inside the harbour, clanking and ringing rhythmically with the surf, I threw a leaf against the wind and watched as it jerked and spun to the slated angles below and disappeared down a chimney.

Bored again by the sight of our tiny seaside village, my attention moved to my wrist. The crusty little mound there was so black that as I rubbed my thumb across it, it seemed it could be no blacker. Perhaps it was a trick of the light. The blazing sun lowering and bouncing off the sea in our direction, making it darker than was possible.

'Nanna's 96 and hers is still grey,' Char boasted.

'*How* grey?'

'Like that car down there.' She nodded to a minivan slowing at a tight bend down towards the seafront.

'That's *silver!*'

'Okay then.' She stopped texting and looked around impatiently for a second, only to huddle the sunlight away from her vibrating phone again. 'I guess it's more like… like this actually,' she decided, cupping her hand around the screen. She pointed to the grey *RETURN* button.

'That's like my Dad's,' I realised.

While she carried on texting, I stared over her shoulder at that dull grey, next to the brilliant white of the space bar. It seemed the true shade of black, white or grey just then could only be determined if it was sitting in contrast with another shade.

'He's only 50,' I mumbled, shrinking away from her.

'My mum told me sometimes you can change overnight,' she said innocently enough. 'Like turn white with a fright or something. Jack's on the hill. Wanna go?'

'Not really.' Realising that's who she was texting, 'He's the last person I want to see,' I insisted. And I was pretty sure he didn't want to see me either, because Jack wanted nothing more than to have Charlotte to himself, to show off without someone standing there beside her, eager to challenge his every lie. Of course what annoyed me most about him was that he couldn't just sit and talk like the rest of us did. He had to prove something. 'Besides, I thought your mum didn't want you hanging around with him this summer,' I reminded.

'I can't be on my *own* with him,' Char clarified. 'So you *have* to come.'

'I don't want to,' I said flatly, rubbing my thumb

over my dot again. 'Remember last time?' How she could even ask me, after Jack chased us off the dunes with a sun-dried rat skewered through a length of bamboo.... Chased *me*.... 'He's sick. He gets his kicks off seeing people squirm and you should block him,' I said firmly, nodding to her phone. Only she didn't see because she was lifting it high up away from me to get a better signal. 'Seriously Char. I'm not spending the entire summer break following you around while you hook up with Jack.'

'It's the first day, Ivy. And I'm only interested this time because he said he just had some really bad news.' She thrust her log of texts into my face as proof knowing I couldn't bear to read his rubbish. 'Now you can sit there and look at *that* all you want,' I flicked my wrist over, pretending I hadn't been looking at anything, '*or come*—because I'm *going*.'

The thought of Jack having any sort of news meant he might actually have something to talk about for a change. Perhaps he was going away for the summer—or *moving* away. A Jack who showed some sort of regret for once... disappointment... now that was a Jack I wanted to see.

'Fine...' I said, rolling my eyes.

We jumped down from the rock overlooking Trebullan, cut through the gravel carpark behind us and took the coastal path along the clifftops. Halfway to the hill, it occurred to me this could be one of his pranks again. A sad-sounding text to oblige us as accomplices for whatever he really had planned.

'Listen, if he wants to go to the farm, I'm going home,' I warned.

'We're not going to the farm. Just stop whinging.'

From the bottom of the golf course, we saw Jack's

lanky body stretched horizontally across the bench on the hill, his red baseball cap set atop his face.

'Seriously Char, if he's up for any pranks…' I called out, watching her hurry ahead into the wind and scramble up the sandy hill by sticking her feet into the entrances of rabbit warrens. 'Seriously… I don't trust him…!'

When I finally caught up to them at the top, Jack was upright on the bench with his head hung low and his arms dangling off his knees. He didn't seem in the mood for pranking anyone and by the look on Charlotte's face, it really was bad news.

'What is it you guys?' I eyed them both, waiting. It seemed Char was giving Jack the chance to say something first, only he wouldn't. 'Seriously, what's the matter?'

Charlotte discreetly turned her wrist over, bulged her eyes at me and then to her mark.

Unsure of what she was going on about, 'Jack, what is it?' I said, bending to his lowered face shaded beneath his cap.

He shoved his wrist in my direction.

The mole there, no bigger than his thumbnail, wasn't as black as I had seen it only the day before. Glossy black like an olive. No, Jack's death dot was like parched slate and very much greyed now. I couldn't help but look at Char's wrist, then caught a glimpse of my own anchored at my knee as I bent down over Jack's. As he snatched it back, there was no doubt, *we* would live longer than he would.

Charlotte put her arms around Jack and I too felt the urge to comfort him. No matter how horrible he had been, he never actually hurt any of us. Not really. He was just bored. A clever lad, bored out of his mind by this nowhere little village. And it was made worse by the influx of holiday crowds with real lives at the start of every summer that mocked us when they left, saying they wish they could stay.

'I'm so sorry Jack,' I said, taking the space the other side of him, putting my hand on his bony back, rubbing. 'I'm so sorry.'

'I don't know what happened,' he confessed, shrinking between us. 'I just woke up and there it was. Like this. It's not like anything happened since yesterday and today....'

'Does anyone else know?' Charlotte asked, wiping an eye.

'My mum. My gran. Apparently it's lighter than *hers*.'

Char looked at me over Jack's back and cringed.

'That's horrible...' she tried soothing, hugging him sideways and pressing her head to his shoulder.

'It is,' I said thoughtfully, realising that only this morning I had seen his mum at the cash point with her bakery uniform on. Just as I was coming to meet Char above the cove. She probably didn't know then. 'She must be devastated.'

'She is. She couldn't get out of bed today.... Couldn't face leaving the house... couldn't face work....' And just as he went on about how he had to get out, how he couldn't stand the wailing... how this changed his entire view of the world, of everyone around him... I slipped my hand from his back, gently took his forearm and stared at his death dot once more. He too was staring at it now, gibbering on. My eyes narrowed at its smooth surface and without even thinking, I spat.

Jack flashed his offended blue eyes at me and yanked his wrist back.

'What's wrong with you?' he accused, rubbing the

spit off on a rib.

'*Now* show me.'

He stole a peek at the dot, checked Char wasn't able to see and then pressed his arm into his side.

'I'm not going to now.'

His playful indignation undermined everything he said to get us onto the hill, get us sitting beside him comforting him.

'It's a prank!' I declared to Char as I shot up off the bench. 'Another of his pranks! Good grief Jack...' I said incredulously, standing over him, 'is there any more to you than *lies...?*' I could feel my hatred infecting Char, forcing her to see what had always been obvious to me. 'You know you're mum didn't look too upset at the *cash point* this morning,' I hastened, '*in her tabbard!*' Furious, I crossed my arms and watched my best friend grab at his hand and inspect the dot for herself. After a second, she chucked his arm back and stood beside me with equal exasperation.

'*What?*' he exclaimed innocently. 'It was a *joke...*' he laughed, hiding a fair number of his freckles in the creases of his cruel smile.

'*Why,* Jack?' Char shouted as the wind from behind us whipped her long blonde hair and sent strands snagging against her lashes. 'I *believed* you....' She jerked her face against the gust and seeing him clearly for a moment demanded, 'What's *wrong* with you?'

Jack clearly had no idea. He made some sort of mocking comment about her shedding a tear for him, so she flicked his cap off, watched it bounce away in the wind and then turned and stormed back down the hill.

'I *knew* it,' I said, a metre behind her, sliding downwards in the sand. 'It looked dusty... like he put something on it. All he does is *lie*—lie and *steal*—and I wouldn't be suprised if it's *him* behind all those thefts up at Churley's....'

'*Enough* Ivy! Just stop talking *okay?*'

'I'm just saying....'

'You're just saying you're *right*—as usual—and I'm tired of hearing it—*as usual*. Now would you just leave me alone?'

Her long legs steadily increased the gap between us around the bottom of the golf course and through the fields. And she didn't wait for me at the style to the road. When I climbed over and saw her silhouette halfway to the village, I decided to go home the long way.

I promptly marched up the road, stomped the entire length of a barley field and forgot how close I was to the farm until I heard the unnerving sound of a child's scream.

All the agricultural land surrounding Trebullan belonged to Churley Farm. It had everything within a 10-mile sweep, including the field sloping over the clifftops of our seaside town like a jaundiced forehead when the rapeseed was in full bloom. The actual farm house sat up there at the highest point like a pale blemish, *oozing all sorts*. Dad's words, not mine. He said Churley hired Transients from June through to October to help with the crops and that we needed to keep our wits about us until they had gone.

The scream came again. This time though, to my relief, it sounded like a shriek of joy. Surprise. And there it was again, accompanied by a two other happy screeches. Like young children were playing a game. Up in the orchard.

I hurried over the next style and took the overgrown path through waist-high rapeseed. It was that, or the dirt track running parallel. At least with the rapeseed, I knew half the town could see me up on the ridge cutting across the forehead. The last thing I wanted was to be alone on that track, out of sight, hidden by high walls of unkempt hawthorn and bramble...

I lifted my knees up through the yellow and let the stiff sheaths and velvet blossoms whip repeatedly against my legs, numbing them as the sounds of child screams became temptingly pleasant. The style was visible there in the distance, and with no obstacles in between, I felt confident I could spot anyone approaching from quite far off.

Just then, the wind shifted and I couldn't hear anything from the farm. However, coming to the end of the field, I hopped from the style onto the north road out of Trebullan and heard something right beside me—a twig *snap*—in the dense hedge.

Peering blankly, I suddenly made out that there was a form there. A tanned face with bright eyes, looking through the hawthorn at me.

'Hey,' he whispered, those teeth so white.

But I ran. Right down the steep streets of Trebullan until I reached home.

Chapter Two

Good-bye

Mum stood at the other end of the hall in front of the mirror and was already pinning her hair up for work when I stumbled through the door.

'Good timing Ivy' she said, focused on the glass. 'Now dinner's on the side...' the pins in her mouth made her sound angry '...and Gran's settled in her room for the night. Give her her meds would you, at 9?'

Red-faced and sweating, 'Yeah,' I said, only slightly out of breath now.

'What happened to you?'

'Nothing. Just thought I'd run down the hill.'

Mum looked at me. All 180lbs of me, and frowned.

'Where's Charlotte?' She removed the last two pins from her mouth then turned back to the mirror.

'Back home.'

'And where have you been this afternoon?'

'The cove. Witch Rock. And then the bench

between the dunes and the golf course.'

'Well don't go out and I don't want you having anyone over.' She patted her bun and looked at it from the side. 'It may be the summer, but visitors unsettle your Gran and she could do with this place being quite a few days.' She came away from the mirror then went through to the next room where she grabbed her mug from the small dining table positioned at the edge of the linoleum that divided the kitchen-diner from the carpeted lounge. 'My shift is over at 6. Any trouble, just ring me.'

'We'll be fine Mum,' I said plainly, getting a drink of water. 'It's not like you've never left us before....'

With her purse already over her arm, she came over to the sink and stared at me with what seemed regret. Or pride. *And* pride, maybe. Probably because she knew it wasn't Gran looking after me anymore, but the other way round. And probably because I remembered when Gran needed her meds when Mum herself often forgot. She probably appreciated too just then that Gran was now frail enough, and I strong enough, to lift and carry Gran wherever she was in the house, alleviating pressure sores and helping with trips to the toilet. Of course, she wouldn't have forgotten either that if anyone could get Gran to eat... it was me.

'You *will* be fine,' Mum agreed, then kissed my sweaty forehead. 'Now don't forget the meds.'

'I know... the green ones, 9 o'clock. Blue before breakfast.'

With that, she quickly pinned her upside-down watch to her uniform and was out the door, off to the hospital.

Gran however wasn't settled when I took her the comfort capsules. She was mumbling away in her chair with the telly on low, looking distressed.

'Gran? ...What is it?' I went and I knelt beside the armchair. 'Gran?'

'There you are,' she said, recognising me. 'I was afraid I'd miss you....'

'Miss me? You won't miss me. I'm right here. I've got these to make you feel better.'

I held out the glass of water and green capsule.

'Mum's just left for work. She's starting a new shift, so I'll be looking after you at night. Here.'

The crepe folds of skin around Gran's mouth stretched apart like a sparrow chick's and I dropped the medicine in.

'There. Have some of this to wash it down.'

Without fuss, her sinewy, mottled hands cupped together. Their blue veins wiggled as though strings tightening her grip to the glass. She finished, then pulled with a distracted agitation at the buttons on her gown.

'Shall we get you ready for bed,' I prompted. 'Brush your teeth... all that. I bet your bed would feel lovely just now.'

A trip to the loo and half an hour later she was under the duvet with the light out.

'Ivy?'

'Yes Gran.'

She waited a moment before answering.

'I'll miss you my Love.'

Her words pinched at my nose and caught in my throat, making my eyes sting.

'Gran, I'm right here,' I said in the doorway. 'And I'll be here to check on you in the morning.'

'Ivy?'

'Yes Gran?'

'I'll miss you most then.'

Tears streamed involuntarily from my eyes, their heat feeling as though strips tearing through my skin. I told her that I loved her, went and kissed her goodnight and left the room.

In the shower though, I cried until the water went cold, until my cheeks no longer felt the heat. I couldn't stop thinking about those times she showed me her dot—her mortality mole—and guessed playfully how many years she had left against the colour scale. Of course, she was always between two shades. I always saw the darker one, but she insisted it was the lighter. But now, there was nothing lighter. *White* was white. And her dot had been white for days.

Charlotte's mum didn't know what she was talking about. A fright didn't white you faster. Some shades came quickly, but only because they were already gaining pace. And you didn't just stay black for 10 years and then turn white overnight because you became a drug addict... or tried to turn someone else's dot white in a fit of rage. You turned white because it was *your* time. And if *they* turned white, it was their time. If you were honest, you would have seen it coming a long way off. And so would they. People tried making connections, but it was a lie to believe differently. Yet people clung to lies. Clung to the idea that they had some sort of control when they didn't. Could avoid the inevitable. But no matter how stupid you were in life, death came at a steady rate. Fast for some, slow for others. Thankfully, Gran's was slow.

Before bed, I took the shade scale and set it on the chest of drawers. Like finding the numbers on a ruler, I slid my arm along the foot length of transparent plastic, working from white to black, looking for the exact shade to match the dot on my wrist.

Black 6.

There were ten shades within *Black*, *Grey* and *White*. 30 altogether. After 16 years (nearly 17), I was approximately halfway through a third of my shades. However long they would last. But whatever the length, it would be longer than Charlotte's, who was already at *Grey 2*. Of course, there's nothing to be done, nothing to determine your years of life, except watch how quickly the shades come and go. But even then, it's not an exact science. Days... hours and minutes... they were like pressing a tape measure to the immeasurable coastline, with all its coves and caves, peninsulas and ever-changing beaches. You had to go to the expensive posh clinics to get an Expected Length of Life fix, but even then, it wasn't exact. Sometimes it wasn't even remotely accurate. There were gene anomalies, minutely stunting and boosting your progress through the shades, and there was always one the labs missed. In fact, the daughter of the billionaire who owned the sweets chain in town sued a clinic for over-estimating her father's life expectancy by two days.

Two days.

Two days short of what the tabloids had declared would be the wedding of a decade. Minus one prominent guest.

Sometimes Expected Length of Life therapy wasn't money well-spent. Though it would be nice to know for certain, I couldn't even say the five shades between Charlotte's dot and mine would be the same in ten years' time, just further along the scale, because her steady increase might be at a rate much faster in years to come. And of course, who was to say I wouldn't pick up speed over the decades and rocket ahead?

Whatever our rate through the shades, the only certainty one had was that brilliant white left you with less than a week. Days... hours or minutes... you made sure things were in order by the time white came. It didn't stop the sadness, but it ensured the end was meaningful. Ensured proper good-byes. They'd be planned. Exactly as you wanted. For the most part.

I cried again for Gran, who would miss me in the morning.

Chapter Three

Dignity

I heard nothing after I knocked. I hoped that coming in earlier might prove her wrong, but she knew. White never lies.

Already, I missed her.

As I sat beside the bed and looked at Gran's peaceful face in the early morning sunrise, I could have sworn her eyelids flickered, but they didn't. It was just a gull flying outside the window in the distance, directly in the line of sunlight, casting a brief shadow over Gran's forehead.

She had what most enjoyed. 25 years of black, 25 of grey, and 25 to white. Mum said on Sunday the rate of change never increased over the years. No genetic anomalies. A steady plod, she said. The most anyone could ask for. The Goodbye Celebration would tire Gran out she said, and we needed to do our best to let her go in peace afterwards. I then watched her re-fill her cup with punch and take another to Gran sitting in the lawn chair, with family playing and chatting around her, and remembered thinking then how strange it would be for everyone to leave in a few hours' time. It would be as if it had already happened. To everyone who attended, it was good-bye. Why then leave a few days for peace—a few days *loneliness* actually, waiting for death to come?

'Because we don't know when it will *be* exactly,' Mum told me later when Gran was inside for her afternoon nap and we were clearing up. 'When white comes, we have to prepare. *Before* white comes, we have to prepare.' She poured the leftover punch with its melted ice into the rose bush. 'This is what she wanted.'

Gran's pale face looked like an angel's in the now golden light of morning. Her hair a halo. We all said our good-byes and admittedly, she didn't want a fuss. She'd of felt my tears last night though.

I texted Mum at work that it had happened. She was already on her way home. For her, there were no tears. Just happy memories.

'Can you call this number Ivy?' she said when she came in. 'I need to get a few things ready.'

An hour later, two kindly men, officious as much as they were empathetic, in white business suits, put Gran in a White Chair—a reclined chair like the ones you had your hair washed in in the salons, only white and on large wheels. Then with the press of a button, automatic fastenings closed around Gran's tiny frame, keeping her upright and in place.

'Dignity,' the shorter of the two men said with finality, pleased that Gran was neither shrinking nor drooping in the chair, despite heading her for the pavement in her night dress for all the neighbourhood to see.

'She wanted to wear her best,' Mum told the taller

of the two men after they wheeled Gran out to the van and came back in with a matching white suede zipped binder. They looked like two sticks of chalk standing there, one half the length of the other I thought as I wondered just then why Mum hadn't put the clothes on Gran herself, or asked me to do it.

'Indeed Madam. My colleague will be happy to take those for you.' Mum passed Gran's blue tea dress, red cardigan and never-been-worn patent leather flats over to the smaller man who had promptly unfolded a clear zip bag with Gran's name on from what seemed out of nowhere. 'Just one document to sign. Permission for us to care for her now.'

'What will you do with her?' I asked, watching Mum scribble without hesitation on the single sheet in the posh binder while the bag of Gran's shoes and clothes zipped slowly beside me.

'We'll scatter your Gran's ashes to sea,' the man said soberly. He looked out the window towards the stranger he just wheeled into the back of his van, pretending to appreciate more than the business Gran's death brought him. 'And we will make sure no one forgets her.'

'We'll set a memorial bench in her name at Point Tar, just as requested,' the smaller of the two added. 'Whatever your wishes, we will arrange,' he promised sincerely, as if anything were possible. Anything but bringing Gran back.

'Our plans are unchanged as of last month,' Mum assured, seeing them to the door.

'Very well then.' The taller stick of chalk passed her a business card. 'This is a reminder that the scattering of the ashes will happen at 4pm on Saturday and the bench will be put in place an hour before.'

'Thank you so much.' Mum said with what seemed relief, then watched them get in the van and drive off down the road. An hour later she was stripping the bed and putting Gran's things in boxes with family names on to distribute to uncles and aunts, cousins and grandchildren. All that was left of Gran's personal things in her room at the end of the day were pictures. Pictures of those she left behind.

Mum slept most of the day away after that and later, when she was making tea, she said it was a strange thing that she was making dinner for two now.

'Mind you, she hardly ate. Like a bird, really,' she admitted, pushing sausages over with a spatula until they were nearly black.

'Sorry Mum, but I don't think I'm hungry tonight,' I realised.

'You sure Love?'

'Yeah.' No matter how much planning we had done for Gran's Good-bye Celebration… nothing seemed to prepare me for the emptiness I felt at the table there knowing the only presence Gran had in the house now was digital. Images on phones and videos on memory sticks. Finite and small compared to the real person I had known, loved and lived with my entire life. I didn't want her to be gone and I didn't want her things to be gone. And I didn't want her bedroom to become a second sitting room. What I wanted was to go back before white—go back before Sunday, because as far as I was concerned, Sunday's celebration was a sham. Something to help the living cope better, or forget easier. None of which was the case.

I put my fork down. 'I'm sure I'll feel better in the morning.'

Upstairs, I set Gran's picture beside my bed and

returned Charlotte's message. She wanted to know how I was feeling:

Okay. I didn't think I'd feel so sad. Mum did so much preparing with Gran I think she must have grieved weeks ago, becasue she hasn't cried at all. It was nice of you to offer to sleep over but I'd rather be on my own tonight. I'll meet you at the Witch after breakfast. I x

After Mum left for work, I took my duvet downstairs and slept in the empty bed.

Chapter Four

Gaps

The hooked nose of Witch Rock pointed towards the sea. I climbed her chin and stuck my feet into the fissures of her cheekbones and found the best seat on the brim of her hat, where leaning back against its point, I spotted Charlotte down on the beach with her purple backpack, making her way to the path towards me.

'How you doing?' she asked five minutes later from the tip of the Witch's nose.

'The same as yesterday I guess. Okay. You?'

'Fine. I brought us a snack. Is your Mum back?'

She climbed up and joined me.

'Yeah. Asleep.'

'Listen Ivy. I didn't mean to storm off the other day.'

'It's okay. It doesn't matter.'

'It does. You were right about Jack. I just... I wanted to give him a second chance.'

'At what? Pranking us?'

We both smiled at each other.

'I don't know about you, but I'm starving,' Charlotte declared, unzipping her bag. 'Wanna Snickers?'

'Go on then,' I said, holding out my hand.

A moment later, we were talking about Mum's way of dealing with Gran's death and how there seemed to be something horribly ironic about the Good-bye Celebration.

'Your Mum sees broken people all the time at the hospital though,' Char pointed out. 'I know no one ever dies there, but she must see all those hours and days they waste being broken... taking all that time to mend... time they could be living life instead of wasting shades away in intensive care.... Maybe all that makes her see white... and grief a bit differently. Efficiently. I don't know. It's certainly better than *my* mum's view of it all.'

Char peeled back the Snickers wrapper and took a bite.

'When you work on the White Wards,' she went on, 'where all the patients have no family... only strangers to celebrate their last days... well all you do is end up focusing on how cruel that last week can be, don't you? The loneliness of it. It's all you see. I think my mum's biggest fear is facing white alone. Facing that last week. Your nan was lucky to have a Good-bye Celebration with family. I mean, there are plenty of people who don't even have a daughter, much less a granddaughter, to look after them right to the end.'

'I guess.'

Though Charlotte meant well, the problem I had wasn't Mum's easy acceptance of death—because we all accepted it the moment we understood our place on the scale. No, my problem was how Mum made the absence of Gran's life seem insignificant when actually, the void felt massive. Shocking. And I couldn't help notice that when Gran's body was carted off by strangers to be disposed of, Mum didn't cry. She didn't look distressed. Instead, she went in almost immediately afterwards and packed Gran's things away. Like she felt nothing at all. Even on Sunday, she just played the happy, obliging hostess while uncles and aunts, cousins and grandchildren looked just as happy, waving out of their windows... pulling away from the curb, certain to never see Gran again.

Perhaps *that's* what made it all so shocking. That life could just carry on. That Gran's void could be filled with Good-bye Celebrations and second sitting rooms.

'I just don't understand how the family doesn't feel anything, Char. Because me... I'm really upset that she's gone.'

'That's normal,' Char soothed. 'Ivy, you *loved* her.... Of course you're going to be sad. Devastated even. But some of these ironic things, things like a celebration, are there to help you *accept* what's going to happen, so this bit doesn't feel quite so bad.'

I swallowed hard and nodded.

'I still think it's trivial though. Waiting for the worst. And celebrating.'

'It's a chance to say goodbye and remember the good things.'

'Yes I know.'

'It's not just a charade....'

I looked at Char gratefully. 'Everything you're saying makes sense. It's just all that preparation... and it still feels like rubbish.'

'I know...' Char sighed as she gave me a sideways hug. 'I know.'

Before I started crying, I suggested we ditch the Witch and go for a walk. Char was unusually agreeable.

It was a cloudless morning, so we took in the views around the headland and looped around the south road out of Trebullan to the north one back in.

'I didn't tell you, but I came this way when you went off the other night and I saw someone hiding in the brambles up here.' I pointed to the gap in the hedge where the style met the road 50 meters or so ahead. 'They whispered *hey* to me.'

Char stopped with eyes wide. 'Oh my god Ivy! Are you *serious*?'

'Yeah,' I shrugged, pretending it was no big deal. 'It was a boy I think. Tanned. There's that middle bit in there that's like a path.' We both stared into the hedgerow. 'See there.' I noticed how trodden the soil was on close inspection. 'It's wide enough for a person. Someone could come all the way here from the farm without even being seen. from the road or fields.'

'You said *tanned*. It was probably a *Transient* Ivy,' Char realised, clearly disturbed by the thought. 'Seriously, promise me you won't go this way again *alone*. ...Now I really *do* feel bad I left you...'

Stunned, she took another look, gripping her long blonde plait away from the brambles.

'Good grief Ivy, the Transients could have grabbed you and no one would even have *known*,' she determined, peering. Her hunched frame then straightened. 'So when you saw him, what did you do?'

'*Ran*. What do you *think* I did?'

She gave me a worried look from over her shoulder, no doubt guessing I must not have gone any great distance at any great speed.

'I ran all the way home—*without* stopping,' I insisted. 'I mean *obviously* I'm okay, aren't I?' I threw my arms out, checking myself over for effect as she carefully poked her head once more between two thorny blackberry vines. 'Of course all that fitness stuff in school about the social benefits of *keeping up...*' I however admitted, 'well all I kept thinking on the way down the hill was *what about getting away?*'

'See there,' she turned and eyed my short, wide body severely, 'keeping up might just save you from a pervert.'

'Yes, the social perks abound' I admitted wryly, rolling my eyes.

Just then, I spotted a longer section of the path there inside the hedge and felt a strange urge to go in. Only there were no gaps this side big enough.

'You're not thinking of going in there I hope,' Char heeded, narrowing her eyes at me. Then flicking her blonde plait over her shoulder, 'I thought we could go to the falls and swim,' she suggested. 'I brought towels and mags.' And a few minutes later, we were wading across the yellow brow of Trebullan, heading for Point Tar, right where Gran's bench would sit in less than a week's time.

Chapter Five

Wanderers

We took the shortcut down from Point Tar and entered the rubble-filled opening to Free Falls from the beach. It was just after we crossed the high mound of loose slate that I heard it first. A third time and Charlotte finally admitted to hearing it too.

We leaned against a massive mound of rock and lifted our ears to the commotion the other side.

'Someone's there. Maybe more than one,' I calculated by the quick succession of splashes. 'It takes longer than that to climb to the top and jump.' Unwilling to meet anyone but friends in such a secluded place, I quickly pushed away from the rock and instead hunkered next to a limp tangle of buckthorn growing out of the base of the cliff. 'Seriously Charlotte, I'm not swimming in my knickers and bra if someone else is there.'

'Well shall we at least see?' she suggested, looking

above me along the narrow path to the stream above. 'Maybe it's Melissa and Georgia. They always come here.'

Careful not to be seen, we abandoned the main opening of the cave and went back onto the beach.

'We can go up that way.' She pointed to the treacherous strip of bare earth maybe a foot wide snaking dangerously close to the cliff edge all the way up to its receded top. 'It'll be fine,' she insisted, ignoring my unsure expression as she began climbing.

Joining her, we found a jutting out point halfway up which allowed us to view into the slanted mouth of the vast cave without entering it. There were more splashes, but neither of us could see anyone. Whoever they were, they were jumping a short distance around the left from where the torrent spilled into the deep clear pool below, and because of this they were just out of our line of vision.

'We need to climb higher,' Char whispered. 'We can look from there.' She pointed to the rock ahead much further out that blocked our view.

A few minutes later, we came to our look-out point, leaned against the precipice on our elbows and slowly poked our heads over the edge towards the falls. There in the pool below was a young boy, maybe five or six with white blonde hair like sea foam, frolicking in the sunlight coming directly through the open ceiling above. Whoever he was with wasn't quite obvious for I skimmed the little beach down there, the rocks either side of the falls and along the main path to the three jumping points, only to find no one else around.

'Surely he's not on his own,' Char determined, screwing up her face at the bobbing head far below us.

'*Ready…?*' A male voice echoed around the cave.

There, opposite us, on a fern-bearded crag, was a boy who looked about our age. He wore black shorts, had sopping hair plastered around his face, and stood at a spot much higher than the other three diving points carved into the cave wall. In fact, he had to be 40-50 feet above the water.

I took in a sharp breath just as Char did. No one ever went from that position—the rocks below couldn't be cleared—the pool wasn't even deep enough if they did clear it.

'Oh my God,' Char whispered, 'he's gonna do it.' She shook her head. 'He's gonna spend *months* in hospital,' she said assuredly as the boy tightened his drawstring and looked down, readying to dive.

He curled his toes over the rock edge, raised his arms, and at that moment, I noticed something against his dark bronze complexion.

'It's white,' I muttered to myself, then told Char beside me, 'his death dot's white. Look,' I nudged.

'*I see you...*' he called out, his white teeth shining. '*You two! Behind the rock there—I see you...!*' He pointed right at us, smiling wide, to which Char and I promptly ducked our heads and gave each other a panicked look. 'Why don't you jump from where you are?' he beckoned. 'It's not shallow....'

Without thinking, we bolted back down the path as the small child below caught sight of us and started clap-splashing and chanting *jump-jump-jump!*

'Hurry!' Char urged, poking my shoulder.

'I *am!*'

We carried on along the beach until our legs felt like jelly and then fell flat on the wet sand, wrapping our arms around our aching bellies.

'I can't believe he *saw* us…' Char gushed.

'I can't believe his dot's *white!*' I burst out. 'I mean… what was he *thinking*?'

After a few minutes, we caught our breath and sat up, concerned.

'Maybe it's one of the last things he wants to do, that dive,' Char considered. 'Mind you, it'll only land him in hospital for the *rest of his days* most likely. What a waste….'

'I just can't believe he encouraged *us* to jump—we'd break every bone in our bodies,' I remarked, thinking that maybe the boy perched along the cave wall had been the same person I saw in the hedge. Those teeth were so white. But all Transients' teeth seemed that white.

'You know he was from the farm Ivy. Maybe he *wanted* us to break every bone in our bodies—to spite us for his own short life.'

'He was looking after a *child*…' I however pointed out the unlikeliness of such a motive, '…he was just being friendly.'

'Friendly?' Char eyed me dubiously.

'Well he seemed… sincere. Like he was trying to be nice.'

'Don't be ridiculous Ivy. That's what they *do*. And that's precisely how they get *free* rent and utilities on *private* land. They come at you all *friendly*… promising labour and all sorts, but then they steal everything lying around and run off, leaving the place a tip.'

She sounded just like Dad.

'Is that true Char,' I challenged, 'is that *actually* what happens, or is that what people are *afraid* will happen, because Churley Farm isn't run by an idiot you know?' I suddenly hated how fearful our little village was of anyone coming in from the outside, anyone coming from somewhere else and staying for longer than two weeks' holiday. 'Mr Briggs was an army general. And a business man after he lost his leg. I can't imagine he'd fall for someone who'd swindle him.'

'I'm just saying....' Char dismissed with a shrug. But she was just repeating what her father told her. Her father who worked in social housing and despised anyone who didn't pay a mortgage like he had to.

'Well, my Dad *just says* too,' I confessed, knowing Char had heard him say the same thing at least a dozen times. 'And I don't trust anything that comes out of his mouth. I mean, we could very well accuse *him* of being a wanderer of sorts, now couldn't we?' I raised an eyebrow, intimating the fact that he had been chucked out last year and was on his own in a cottage on the moors because he cheated on Mum twice. 'It's quite possible the thing he hates in others is simply the thing he hates about himself,' I said pointedly.

'Well whatever Ivy,' Char dismissed, unzipping her bag. 'I don't care if it was your dad or mine. Whatever that lot from the farm intend to do here, the bottom line is *stranger-danger*—no matter how cute they are!' She threw me suggestive eyes, letting me know what she thought of the boy at the falls as she pulled water bottles out for us both.

'Not him too,' I sighed, annoyed. 'George... Toby and Jack... since *May*. And now *him*?'

'Oh get a grip. It's not like anything's going to *happen*....' She glugged half her drink, then exhaled with great satisfaction as she screwed the top back. 'Seriously, I don't think we need to worry about seeing those guys again. They *avoid* locals like at all cost. The only reason we were invited to join them was because they knew they shouldn't have been there in the first place. The last thing they wanted was to be seen as *scaring* us off.'

I took a drink and suddenly realised that's exactly what had happened. We ran off like they *had* scared us.

The thought of being involved in any village rumour surrounding Transients made my stomach shrivel.

'Why are you looking at me like that?' Char demanded playfully. 'Seriously Ivy, I was just joking about fancying him. *Stranger-danger,* remember?'

She took our bottles and stuffed them into her bag while I wished I had done something different back at the cave. Not run, at least. Or said no thank you even. Anything that might have given assurance *we* weren't the bad guys.

'You still look worried,' she said, gauging me. 'It was the whole hedge thing, wasn't it? Listen, you don't need to be stressed out by them Ivy. That whole group up there'll empty the orchards, pack it all up for the supermarkets and be off by the end of summer... and all we'll hear of them once they're gone are the stories about how they outstayed their welcome.' She got up, slung her bag over her shoulder then added, 'And that bloke back there, you don't need to worry about him either. He'll be practically invisible now we ran away.'

Her confident words made me feel guilty somehow.

Chapter Six

Madame Laurent

We headed for Madame Laurent's on the seafront. It was a little ice-cream spot with walls squeezed into the gap of an alley to keep the storms a hundred years ago from washing up the village backstreets. *The Plughole*, locals still called it, despite Madame's chic tourist-grabbing sign fixed firmly over the chiselled Victorian christening.

'I asked last time, it's your turn,' Char reminded.

Reluctantly, I went in and stood beside the sugar and cream sidetable until the queue shortened. When there were only two people waiting, I got in behind them.

'Ah… Madame Moore… Come to collect my cups and serviettes and plastic spoons,' Madame Laurent declared in her softened French accent when I hesitated to give her my favourite choice of ice-cream. She closed the freezer chest and wearily blew a strand of hair slipping down from her untidy, greyed bun, suggesting the last thing she wanted to do was pick up shop litter from the curb outside.

'Have we come at a good time,' I cringed, hoping.

'You come at a very good time! As usual Ma Chérie.' She reached for a bin bag under the till and handed it over. 'I will sell little this afternoon when the rain comes in. And the napkins out there will be as soggy leaves. *Please...* collect away.' She flapped her hands towards the sea, encouraging. 'Mint Marshmallow Chocolate will be waiting when you return.'

'She never says no to you,' Char complained, slouched against the bollard, having spotted the bag in my hand. 'She's said no to me like twenty times,' she exaggerated, texting again.

'I'm not doing this on my own you know,' I reminded pointedly, waiting for her to put her phone away.

'Done in a minute.' After a few seconds, Char pocketed the device and stood up. 'I saw a little whirlwind behind the bins down that way with loads of *Hot Drinks and Iced Indulgences* stuff on. You pick it up and I'll hold open the bag.' And before I could protest, she pointed out that I held the bag last time.

'Fine....'

We started with the commercial bins the south side of the seafront and worked our way back up to the start of the one-way system the other end, watching the weather change dramatically from cobalt skies and skin-itching sunshine in those 45 minutes to achromatic plumes with ashy slants roving towards us from far out at sea. All the while, Char kept getting out her phone and checking it.

'Who is it?' I asked, annoyed, only to realise from

her evasive response that it was probably Jack. 'Please tell me it's not him,' I begged.

'It's not him,' she said sarcastically, obviously lying.

We skimmed shop steps and entrances once more either side of Madame Laurent's then stood out in front of *Iced Indulgences*.

'What flavour?' I asked as Char handed me the bag and dug out her phone again. I exhaled impatiently while she read a text and screwed up her face. '*Hel-lo…?*'

'Actually Ivy… my mum wants me home now. I've gotta head back.'

'And she was gone, just like that,' I told Madame Laurent half an hour later as wind crackled rain against the long, narrow windows so fiercely, it blotted out the deserted seafront. 'She's always doing this, leaving me,' I sighed as a blurred, hunched form caught my eye darting along the pavement outside. 'One minute we're having a nice time, and the next, she gets a text and's gone.'

Madame Laurent came to the tiny table with hot chocolates and sat opposite me, listening as I told her what I always did. However this time she seemed more interested. More concerned. And after my drink cooled a bit, I resigned myself to the inevitable cycle of falling-out-with-Char and sipped.

'Ivy, it is no small thing, friendship. It is impossible without honesty and compromise. These trials, they are… opportunities to nurture what you have with this Charlotte.'

'Yeah well, *opportunity* sounds positive, doesn't it? But there's nothing positive about how I feel right now.'

Then delicately, 'Perhaps your grandmother's absence has something to do with that?' Madame Laurent suggested. She then looked at me sideways with an empathic frown.

'Maybe,' I said, quickly diverting to the inside of my mug as I sipped.

'How are you feeling about her absence?'

'Fine. I guess. I'm a bit angry though that people have forgotten her already.'

'Forgotten her? In what way?'

I let the mug hover between us, like a little barricade, knowing Madame Laurent wouldn't like what I was about to lob at her.

'Well like before she even died, when we had the big celebration, people were preparing to forget her while she was still around. None of them intended to come back—none of them *came* back—and she was still alive for at least another few days. It was like they couldn't bear to see her that white —that close to death—so they didn't bother. Which makes the whole party a charade then, doesn't it? Coming to say good-bye, knowing it's not really, but just getting it done and over with.' I rolled my eyes, thinking how there had only been a few people who actually even interacted with Gran that day. The rest just busied themselves around her, talked about her like she wasn't even there... or talked about everything else just the same. 'No one mentioned her dying. It was like a birthday party or something.'

Madame Laurent hesitated before saying anything and took a breathy swig from her overly creamed hot chocolate. After a moment, she licked froth from her top lip then said thoughtfully,

'Death is all around us Ivy. Always present in our minds. From the moment we position ourselves on the scale. Yet when it comes into our own homes... takes something from us, none of us is quite prepared.

Even when we go through the motions of accepting it, through the celebrations that help us to do so... it will always be the unwelcome consequence of life.'

'Unwelcome?' I put my mug down. 'If it's so unwelcome, why is Mum already looking forward to changing Gran's bedroom into a second sitting room? It's not even been a *week*,' I remarked sourly, draining the kind expression from Madame Laurent's face. 'And if it's such an unwelcome consequence of life, why isn't anyone acting like Gran's death is some great loss? She died alone,' I said angrily. '*Alone.* No one was there.... Mum went off to work like it was just another shift... I was too afraid to stay in the room with her... We both knew it was going to happen but I didn't want to see her die....' I took in a deep breath and felt the heat of a tear rolling down my right cheek. 'Obviously *no one* wants to see that,' I confessed, my indignation forcing me to swipe away the tear, 'but then they could at least stop acting like it never even happened—like she died when the Good-bye Celebration ended... because now... now it just feels like I'm the only one who knows she's really dead.... What was the whole point even of that stupid thing anyway?' I demanded bitterly. '*Good-bye Celebration*.... It's a *joke*. A con. An easy out for those who can't be bothered to see a loved one to the end.'

Madame Laurent expelled a puff of air from her lips as though at a loss. She then gave my wrist there on the table a brief squeeze and said confidently, 'My Darling Ivy, your grandmother and I were good friends. When her mole turned white, she did not want to become a burden to anyone. She would not have wanted you next to her in the end for the same reason you could not bring yourself to *be* there. She made it quite clear to me that the most important thing near the end was that she didn't want to cause anyone pain. And I can assure you, death is painless, yet we make it painful worrying about its effect on others. So while you might see the Good-bye Celebration as a mockery, it was the necessary gathering to free us... free those of us who stay behind to accept what is coming... frees the one leaving to embrace death as everyone else must. And it is not that everyone is impatient for death to come, or apathetic. It is that they are trying desperately to accept it. Accept that in the shadow of it, life is still there to enjoy. Because as you know, *reach 10 of White, and you could go any night.*'

Madame pursed a well-meaning smile.

'The gathering makes the most of what little time there may be,' she went on. 'And I know for a fact that Mary wanted to see all her family before she went. But she most certainly did not want them all there beside her during her last breaths,' she shrugged. 'She didn't want anyone there. So you mustn't feel guilty she was alone in the end. She wanted it that way. All of us who have lived long lives prefer it that way. To go quietly. Think instead of how lucky you were to have had those few extra days with her no one else had. I of course think about my last cup of tea with her the afternoon before she died. So you and I... we have been given a privilege. Those who saw her only at the celebration... it is true, they missed out. But you and I... your mother... we *were* with her to the end, and rightly so. Who else would she have wanted?'

I hadn't thought of it like that, and took another sip.

'The Good-bye Celebration is essential,' Madame insisted, looking to some point mid-air to her left. 'It is an incredibly brave thing for all involved to have to do when white is near. But we all must do it. The living and the dying. We all must be brave.'

Somehow, using Gran's own phone to text everyone that her dot had turned white and then putting a few tables out on the lawn... a bit of food... topped up tea and coffees... didn't seem so brave.

'You do not look convinced,' Madame gauged me.

'I don't know.' I couldn't help think of the men in white with their wheely chair, and Mum signing Gran off like an old sofa to be recycled. 'I just wish I wasn't the only one feeling sad.'

'My Darling Ivy... I can assure you... I have scooped ice cream all day and still the only thing I feel is sad. Your Gran was my closest friend.'

As I watched Madame blink rapidly and hide her nose into her drink, for she was clearly trying not to cry, it occurred to me that others who knew Gran *had* to be sad. That maybe they went about their business simply because death was *too* sad. Because if they didn't, they'd never do another thing until the feeling subsided. And who knew how long that would be.

But they could at least talk about it.

Like Madame was.

Maybe that's why I was angry at them.

'Gran's ashes will be scattered on Saturday at 4pm,' I suddenly remembered. 'And the bench goes up an hour before.'

'Yes Ivy. I know.'

Just then, a man who looked about Madame Laurent's age, in his fifties, came into the shop. He kept his head down and made minimal eye contact with Madame, making it clear he wasn't interested in hot drinks or ice-cream. In fact, he was underdressed for the weather, in a vest, shorts and Velcro sandals, and he was wet through and heavily tanned.

A Transient, no doubt, from the farm.

At that moment, I thought of the boy who called out to us at the falls as Madame Laurent excused herself and returned to the counter, greeting the man pleasantly as she went. She offered him a complimentary drink, only to appear disappointed at his polite refusal. A minute later, a second customer came in and ordered a coffee, so I slipped out and headed for the library up the hill in the old church building where I knew neither Charlotte nor Jack would ever be seen.

Chapter Seven

Break

As the rain pelted me from behind, I couldn't stop thinking about the boy at the falls, with his gingersnap skin, brandishing that white dot.

'Afternoon Ivy.'

'Afternoon.'

Mrs Weedle watched me pinch at my soaked t-shirt just inside the entrance.

'Is mum on nights again?'

'Yeah,' I said, passing her on the reception desk. 'I thought I'd come and look at the magazines.'

'You go on ahead, Love. You're the only one here. I'll be closing at 2pm today.'

'Thanks.'

Half wet, half dry, I went straight for the white locker unit in the back with magazines on the door fronts and back issues in the cubby spaces behind. I spotted *Vogue*, *Cosmopolitan*, *Bazaar*, grabbed the latest issues and sat with their glossy covers lined up next to one another at a table nearby.

Here, *Versace*, *Dolce & Gabbana*, crystal-embellished *Valentino*... they weren't what caught my eye and would come to mind later when I'd have to clean the bathroom or hang the laundry. No, here, where a bend in the binding created a gap between the pages and lifted them from one another so my finger could find the place I had visited at least three times a week this last month easily, I found the snake pit of a dozen or so pale bodies, all shapes and sizes, oiled and pressed against one another. Their hands were held in prominent poses to the camera, languid and open-palmed atop some nearby limb, torso or back, and each displayed a unique style of diamond bracelet that shimmered in magnificent contrast to the blackest death dots I had ever seen on adults. I wanted to believe it was possible, that black like this was real. However, these were supermodels. Super men and women with super earning and spending. They were caught in the other magazines up to all sorts.

I glanced up at the celebrity tabloids on the locker opposite, seeing the same prominent model contorting beside my elbow under baseball cap, sunglasses and hoodie, pushing through a mob of photographers with substance abuse accusations in the headlines. Surely someone with the blackest of dots wouldn't carry on like that. I had heard that people became careless when they neared white, taking the risks they hadn't dared to when they were heading well into the greys. (The greys had that effect on you, reminding you of your mortality.) However the picture here... that oily-olive black... maybe that's why they were so careless. Because they had all the time in the world. Certain I would never meet any adult that dark, part of me wanted to believe those perfect diamonds set atop those anaemic wrists, those Black 1 wrists, was just make-up.

I thought of Jack just then, with simple chalk dust, getting Char to come at a moment's notice, dragging me behind her.

I thought too of gingersnap and white.

Surely a Transient wasn't trying to break, I told myself. Not *that* close to white.

I pictured the Transient boy there on his fern-adorned crag, chin up, arms out, like some crucified god. White like a headache tablet.

My face lifted from the page to the accusations on the lockers. *Work Avoidance: Super Model Super Stressed... Agency Drops Delinquent Beauty... Hospital or Lost-it-all: How Broke is Broken—You Decide!*

What if he *had* been trying to break? What if a week of white meant danger was no obstacle? I looked back to diamonds and dots, shimmering white and black, still seeing those arms outstretched above the falls.

The young boy in the water below... he would have struggled to get back to the farm for help if the dive happened—he might even have gotten lost. The thought of the little guy being delayed, wasting all that time... while someone was lying there broken, waiting to be mended...waiting to die.

I closed the magazine, unsure as to whether Mum and her colleagues at the hospital even tried mending you when you were already *White 10*, and chucked everything back into the lockers. I said goodbye to Mrs Weedle, entered a patch of radiant sunshine and went straight for the beach. The slants of rain were still heading this direction, but the tide was out far enough. The beach was quicker to the falls than taking the clifftop paths or cutting through the fields and I knew I could be at the cave in 15 minutes, well before the tide came up.

I ran a bit more than halfway when my lungs began to tighten painfully. Instead, I strode along quickly, hopped over a stretch of rock pools and came to where the stream off the golf course met the sea. Here, as I ran through the cold fresh water spilling onto the beach, I glanced up the shrubby ravine and saw two figures walking in the direction of Trebullan along the same path Char and I had taken days before to meet up with Jack. I thought for a fleeting second the two forms there were those from the falls, the older and younger boy, that they were heading back to the farm and nearly halfway by the look of it. Only, as I stopped ankle-deep in the pebbly gully in the sand, the red cap was a dead giveaway.

Instantly my shoulders fell, because right behind Jack was someone with a long plait draped over the shoulder, holding what looked like a mobile phone high up to get the best signal.

I narrowed my eyes at Char and clenched my teeth.

Quickly, before they had a chance to spot me, I carried on in the opposite direction to the sand banks well out of sight to the falls.

Chapter Eight

Truth

The heavy rain of an hour ago transformed the falls into a spectacular torrent and added another meter to the pool's depth. I climbed a few rocks around to the left to get a higher perspective but saw no one. Finding myself alone, the shaded walls of the cave felt mysterious. Dangerous. Like they were hiding something amid their dark crevices. Yet the sun streaming over the pool there, revealing clear, calming water at the edges, felt as though a defiant invitation. I had never been here on my own before. And being here now felt as though I had cut some leaden chain fastened between Char and me.

I could have secrets too, I told myself. *I didn't need her to—*

'So are you going to jump in or what?'

Startled, I looked around. The deep voice echoed around the cave, calling from all directions it seemed.

'Up here....' He looked down on me from the

safety of the path at the top of the falls. 'What's it gonna be?' The Transient encouraged me off my rock, throwing his arm indiscriminately to the pool, presenting it, revealing his white dot again.

'I was just looking for someone,' I called out over the rush of the water.

'The girl who was with you before? I just saw her off with that bloke in the red hat. They went that way.' He chucked a thumb over his shoulder and added, 'You just missed them.'

Pretending to be a bit annoyed by that fact, I rolled my eyes and jumped to a rock behind me as if to leave.

'I wouldn't go that way—the tide's coming in.' His concern caught me. 'Come up this way.'

As I hopped across the slate boulders to the sliver of path Char and I had used only hours before, I realised halfway up to the top that the younger boy had disappeared. Unnerved by this, I quickly found a short-cut and climbed to where I could see the entire cave from bottom to top and the majority of the paths down into it.

There he is.

He was wading waist-deep through the torrent at the top of the falls alongside the huge log fixed across the gap. It seemed he was heading over to where Char and I had seen him before. And that must have been how he got so high for his dive, by crossing the fall.

'Is that safe?' I shouted.

'I left my hoodie,' he pointed across to the little ledge where a mound of faded green fabric had been shoved into a crack.

By the time I reached the main path the top, he had reclaimed the item and was already grappling his way beside the log towards me.

'What happened to the little guy?' I asked, watching him jump from the bank of the rushing stream onto the path. He was much taller than I had realised. And I appreciated just then why Char fancied him. His eyes were a pale green. Against his heavily tanned skin, they stood out like gemstones, rolling around in his head as though jade marbles.

'Billy?' He looked over my shoulder in the direction of the farm and indicated with his chin, 'His sister came and got him earlier.'

I watched for a moment while he used his hoodie to dry his head of wavy brown hair. And as he did so, his face changed shape all of a sudden.

'It *was* you...' I realised. 'In the hedge.'

I didn't mean to think it aloud. And I certainly didn't mean for it to sound so accusing.

'I should be going,' he decided, brushing past me up the path.

'*Wait*.... I'm not cross... I just realised, that's all.'

But he didn't look back.

I hurried to catch up with him.

'Seriously, you don't have to go!' I yelled, finding the distance between us stretching as it had done a thousand times with Char. I knew immediately the point at which it would be useless to try and catch up. 'I *liked* talking to you...' I shouted when I knew he was still just within hearing distance.

He carried on a few more paces, leaving me to slow to a stop and it was when I thought he'd disappear behind the dune that he turned to me.

'You like talking to me?' He didn't need to shout. The wind was in my favour.

'That's what I said,' I panted, hurrying to reach him. 'I tend to tell the truth.'

He looked me up and down, apparently drawing the same conclusion.

'It was me in the hedge,' he admitted openly. 'But I wasn't trying to scare you. I'd been setting rabbit traps. Catching food. In fact, I didn't even know you were there until I saw you looking in at me. At that point I decided to say something,' his eyes wafted, loathing, 'because of course, saying nothing *would* have been weird, like I *was* spying on you or something.'

I realised just then how it might have looked to him when my face peered deeply into the brambles.

'Well I wasn't trying to spy on *you*,' I declared with slight indignation. 'I'd just come across the field and heard a noise in the hedge—a twig snap—so I decided to see what it was.'

He stared at me dubiously for a moment.

'You ran though.'

'Because I thought you were trying to watch me...' I said frankly, not bothered now if that had been the case.

'—Well I wasn't.'

'Yes, well I know that *now*.'

He appeared to accept this, then averted his eyes from me to the sea.

'You should get back. Rain's coming in. I can walk you to the road that way if you want.'

As we crossed the bottom of the golf course and stomped through the overgrown fields, we talked about the harvest, how long the farm needed the extra hands for and where the group would be off to next once labour opportunities were exhausted in the area. He said he was 17, home-schooled and worked two hours most term-time evenings driving a forklift.

'I move palettes into store,' he said at the style where I had spotted him in the hedge. He then showed me where the gear shift on the forklift in his last job gave him a thick callous across the palm. I however couldn't help notice his dot. 'Driving keeps me out of the sun, and it's a lot better than picking and packing.' He caught me staring at his wrist and quickly dropped his hand.

'Sorry—I didn't mean to—'

'Doesn't matter,' he said flatly.

'Can I ask you... sorry... but do you not have a dot?' I said curiously, having seen something there I didn't quite understand.

'I do.' He hesitated, '...I did...' then held out his palm again. The white there, the white I thought had been his death dot... *wasn't*.

'Oh my gosh....' I stepped closer, inspecting. 'You haven't got one.... I've never seen someone without one. But it's white....'

'It's a scar.'

'A *scar*?' All I could think was how unfortunate he had been, to have an accident that took away his only indicator of death, and ironically left him white. 'What happened?'

'Just got sliced off.' He shrugged as if it were no big deal.

'Does it not bother you that you don't know?'

'Listen,' he said uncomfortably, glancing over his shoulder up towards the farm, 'I really need to head back.'

'Sure... okay.' I took a step back from his hand and watched his lean frame slip effortlessly past blackberry vines and into the hedge. 'That's fine... but what's your name?' I looked at him expectantly, hoping he would tell me as he turned and faced me through the bramble like he had the first time.

'Theodore. You can call me Teddy.'

'...Teddy. I'm Ivy.'

'I know.' He smiled kindly, leaving me to wonder how he could know such a thing. 'Listen. If you want to meet at the falls again, we'll be there tomorrow. Every day this week hopefully. '

Flattered, I defaulted into suspicion.

'*We?*'

'Me...Billy.'

That young boy shouting *jump* when Char and I saw him before wasn't in the least threatening now.

'What time?'

He gauged the sky, the sun escaping only momentarily from the cloud cover to the waves below. 'Morning. 8 or 9.'

I said okay without even thinking and watched him slink off through the hedgerow until the bends and dips obscured every bit of him. It was only when I found myself alone that I wondered again how he knew my name.

Chapter Nine

Phone

The house smelled of overdone fish fingers and chips when I went in.

'Ivy…? Is that you?'

Who else was it going to be? Certainly not Gran.

'Yes, it's me….'

'I've just come out of the shower… would you get the trays out of the oven… I smell charcoal…!'

'Yes… sorting it…' I called up the stairs, seeing Mum's towelled shape dash across the landing. I dished up for two and started without her.

'I thought we could eat together tonight,' She said disappointedly, appearing in the doorway with her hair dripping water on the shoulders of her uniform as she held her make-up bag.

'Sorry.'

But I didn't stop, and instead loaded peas onto my fork.

'Don't worry.' She sat opposite me and put her bag

beside her plate. 'I just thought that maybe this could be our time together before I head off for work from now on. Seeing as I'm such a zombie in the day, sleeping most of it away.'

I threw her a curt smile and stabbed a chip, appreciating only slightly that she was making an effort to do something with me on a regular basis.

She then added delicately,

'I thought as well that when you're out, even though I'm here, I could give you Gran's mobile.'

'Okay.'

'You wanted a phone for ages and—'

'—We couldn't afford it... I know.'

Deflated slightly, she seemed to think better of insisting we have dinner together.

'Ivy I want to know that you're okay, that's all.'

'Alright.'

'And with Gran gone, I don't want you to feel alone.' She picked up her knife and fork and cut a fish finger in two. 'At least with the phone you can call me from wherever you are. Day or night. And if I'm worried about you, I can ring you.'

'You never worried about me before.'

She looked afraid that I thought as much.

'Yes, well I worry about a lot of things these days.'

We said nothing after that, aside from good-byes. At some point, the phone appeared on the table next to my plate, probably when I was getting water and she was putting her shoes on in the hall. After she left, I took it upstairs to my bedroom after she left and flicked through the contacts list. Most of it was departments at the hospital, the doctor, Mum and Madame Laurent, the ladies who ran the hall and Gran's little trio at the charity.

Coming out of the list I noticed there were texts. Texts to Madame. Texts to Mum. And to someone with only a number, no name.

With Gran gone, it didn't seem so intrusive looking....

Gran: *Thank you for coming Camille. The celebration was divine. I feel there is nothing to hold me back going any day now.*

Madame Laurent: *It was a great pleasure. Anything my dearest.*

Gran: *I would have liked to know I was leaving Pauline and Ivy a bit closer. I worry what Ivy will use to fill the gap I leave. My fear is her mother will work harder and Ivy won't just lose her Gran, but her mother as well. Their relationship is so fraught. 16 demands empathy, compassion, when it has little to give.*

Madame Laurent: *Ivy has always shown you the upmost compassion. Death is difficult at such an age.*

Gran: *Difficult at 75 too!*

Madame Laurent: *Indeed. I will do my best to alleviate your worries my dear friend. Perhaps Ivy can help at the shop? An hour a day might fill a small gap?*

Gran: *I will suggest it to Pauline. I will suggest too that she not leave her alone so often. I had a word with the girls on the committee to keep an eye out over the summer.*

Madame Laurent: *Good idea.*

I stopped there, realising Mrs Weedle in the old

church building knew Gran from the charity, knew somehow Mum had started nights again. I carried on.

Gran: *Will ring in the morning if I'm still around.*
Madame Laurent: *Hoping so. Will come and bide the time with a cup of tea if you're that impatient!*
Gran: *That would be lovely. No fuss.*
Madame Laurent: *Wouldn't dream of it. Customer....*

It ended there.

I had no idea Gran was worried about me.

Mum's comment at the table hit me suddenly and I realised that it might be difficult for her, obliged to go to work as if nothing had happened because death couldn't just keep the rest of us from living. She had to have missed her own mother, but what could she do about it? Surely she wanted to comfort me. But of course, I wouldn't let her.

I regretted just then how cold I had been at the table. The last thing I wanted to do was dislike Mum for what she wanted to change but couldn't.

A lump filled my throat like a little bubble of water and eased its way up and out through my eyes. With tears streaming down my face, I texted mum for the first time. It wasn't on behalf of Gran like all the times before. It was from me, me only:

Dinner will be nicer tomorrow. We'll have pasta a peas and pesto. Ivy

She sent something back almost immediately:

I can't wait. Love you so much. xxx

I wiped my cheek and looked at the next message on the log, the nameless one, feeling a huge weight had lifted from me. All it was was a date and a place. Perhaps it was about the memorial bench, because the date was Saturday, and the place, right where it was going to be erected.

I looked at the last texts, between Gran and Mum. It occurred to me that perhaps Mum knew these texts were here, that she wanted me to find them.

> **Gran:** *It's happening Pauline.*
> **Mum:** *Shall I come?*
> **Gran:** *Please don't.*
> **Mum:** *Do you want me to ring and get Ivy?*
> **Gran:** *No. I'm not afraid. I feel distant.*
> **Mum:** *I love you Mum. I'll miss you.*
> **Gran:** *I love you too.*

These were Gran's last words. To her daugher. I couldn't get the thought out of my head that she had been in her room, waiting. Aware. Maybe even scared. She had looked so peaceful later when I found her.

I didn't sleep in Gran's room that night. Her bed went to someone else in the family, someone I heard her agreeing at the Good-bye Celebration that they could have when she was gone. I couldn't blame Mum for that. And to be honest, I didn't want to sleep in it again.

Chapter Ten

Contagious

I heard the key in the lock just after 7:30am.

'Good morning,' Mum said, pleasantly confused. 'What's this?'

She looked just as surprised to see the mug of tea I was holding out for her as she was to see me up and dressed this early for the summer break.

'Tea.'

Grateful, she leaned against the counter and glugged.

'This is so lovely Ivy,' she gushed, wearily mentioning how short-staffed the night had been, that she had to skip every tea and coffee break. 'Except this one.' Half of her face disappeared into the mug again and I noticed how the fluffy clean hair she left the house with the night before had since turned greasy, leaving her fringe matted across her forehead. And the delicate skin around her eyes appeared as plump blackberry-stained swags. 'I'm exhausted...' she breathed, thanking me and then setting her mug into the sink. 'I'm afraid it's shower and sleep.'

'Well, I'll go out for the morning, maybe go to the falls or something,' I said tentatively.

'Not alone I hope. Tell Char you two need to stick together when you go there.'

'I will,' I lied. The last person I wanted to talk to today was Char.

'Alright Love. Keep your mobile on., will you?' Clearly relieved to be home and dazed with fatigue, Mum peeled off her uniform, dropped it beside the washing machine and moved leaden-legged to the stairs. These night shifts seemed harder on her than last time.

'I will,' I said after she passed by without a word and got all the way up to the landing. She no doubt forgot what she had just said to me, what I was answering for even.

'Oh,' she said absent-mindedly, '...thank you for my tea Ivy... I really appreciated it.... It was lovely.'

Then seeing her disappear to her room, 'Don't forget I'm making dinner,' I called up. 'I'll be back before 4.'

There was a muffled moan of appreciation as her body sounded like it hadn't made it to the shower and instead fell flat onto the bed. I grabbed my backpack and headed straight for the falls.

Despite what Dad insisted, not all Transients were liars. Teddy was there just like he said, and the little boy Billy was there too, his bobbling head cackling with approval at having just been thrown into the pool.

I climbed higher away from the splashes as

Teddy pulled the gangly little blonde boy up onto a rock again and pushed him off once more.

'Is he your brother ?' I asked, sitting down, guessing they weren't on account of the contrasting hair colour between the two.

'He is,' Teddy answered.

I immediately paid closer attention to his brother's facial features and compared them. Of course they were brothers.

'Come up this way Bill,' Teddy instructed, priming his sibling for another go. Just then, as I watched those little arms clamber against the buoyancy of his flotation vest across the water, I spotted something I hadn't seen before. Only, not on that tiny face.

Billy was white too.

'He has a scar like yours,' I blurted without even thinking, prompting a distracted glance from Teddy as he grabbed his brother's hand, pulled him up then pushed him back in again, only with less force this time.

I realised all of a sudden that such a coincidence as two scars—such an accident, happening twice within a family—was probably unlikely.

'*Is* that a scar?' I said quietly as Billy frolicked and floundered for a moment under the surface.

But Teddy said nothing. I could tell he heard me but didn't want to answer.

'Billy... Sarah's coming to take you to the donkeys in 10 minutes. It was just a short trip today, remember? Did you hear...?'

A squeaky *yep-I-heard* spluttered from beneath our rock.

'Come on then—two more goes and then we need to meet her at the top.'

I sat there for the next five minutes trying to get a good look at Billy's wrist, half-hoping all the Transients had scars, but his slender knobbly limbs were just a blur. And the more I stared, the more it seemed a trick of the light. I then wondered if Teddy's evasive reaction was because I had mentioned white when maybe his family didn't. It would have been perfectly understandable that they all downplayed it on account of Teddy's own accident... because he would never see white coming without a mortality mole. Because his little brother would never know how long Teddy would be around.

I thought I understood just how indiscreet I had been, but when Teddy came back down from the top of the falls after handing his brother over to their older sister, the first thing he said was,

'No. It's not a scar.'

'Not a scar...?' I didn't understand.

And then I did.

All I could feel was dread for Teddy as he sat down beside me on the rock.

'Ugh... I'm so sorry.... I-I....' I didn't know what to say. '...How old is he?'

'Six.'

'Good grief,' I breathed, feeling my spine give. 'I've never met a young person with...' I thought aloud, shocked, only to see that Teddy had been staring off towards the other side of the cave and was now closing his eyes, weary-like. 'I'm sorry,' I said once more, remembering myself, determined this time to be delicate. 'When did it—'

'—Two days ago. It turned the day before yesterday.'

That would mean his little brother was nearly halfway through his week of white. No one ever went the last day of their week, the seventh. A week was an over-estimation anyway Mum told me once. Because the transisiton from *White 9* to *White 10* was sometimes missed. Saying a week made true white sound generous. But it never was.

'I'm really sorry Teddy. What an awful situation. You're obviously making the most...' I started to say, referring to his time here with his brother, but before I could finish, I saw his eyes roll, like he didn't want to talk about any of it. Of course he didn't want to talk about how he was spending his last moments with his little brother, here at the falls. Just like I didn't want to talk to anyone about Gran. I thought just then of my last night with her, incapable of imagining her never to wake in the morning. Incapable of making her wake when I found her. I hadn't cared to talk about the night before or the morning of with anyone until that moment on the rock with Teddy.

'My Gran turned white last week,' I admitted quietly. 'She died a few days ago.'

Teddy inhaled deeply, offended like. It occurred to me what I had said, and it hadn't even crossed my mind that an old person and a child turning white were two different things.

'I know it's not the same,' I tried explaining, 'but I wasn't trying to—' but it seemed I was making it worse. 'There's nothing to be ashamed of, telling me,' I assured, wishing I hadn't said anything about Gran at all.

We sat silently for a minute on the rock, shoulders angled away from one another.

'When people find out, they act like it's *contagious* or something,' Teddy said through clenched teeth all of a sudden. 'They *assume* something's wrong with you if you're young and white.'

'I don't think you're contagious,' I offered plainly. 'And I didn't mention my Gran to point out how old she was compared to your brother and try and make you feel bad. I mentioned her because I know how it feels to lose a close family member.'

But however I tried to explain myself, it didn't take away the fact that he was right. People assumed early white meant something was wrong with you and your family. If you were young, in the end shades, they couldn't help see you as a liability. Contagious, just as Teddy said. Thankfully, children got a degree of compassion during their short lives, because they were seen as innocent, barely experiencing life enough to merit death in the first place. They were going before their time. But teens well on their way... young adults, those in their early 20's... they were pitied and shunned until white came and took them, unable to find friends and lovers for fear there was a 50/50 chance such a demise might be passed on to unlikely offspring. In fact, as soon as that red flag started waving—those shades of grey lightening, prompting the inevitable social and emotional decline towards white—a person wouldn't even dare get close enough to become friend... much less significant other, investing, only to lose it all in who-knows-how-long. I never understood this, because those who faced the dreaded white in their 30's and 40's... well it was the opposite. People suddenly saw you as *brave*, securing love and friends when you had limited opportunities. The world had compassion for you somehow, watching you cram in a career, love, a family possibly, despite the inevitable. Of course, if your mortality mole whitened when you were older… say in your 50's upwards, well then you were just lucky. Probably had the best genes or something. It was no wonder that with everyone putting equal value on age as they did shade, the posh clinics wouldn't even see you for Expected End of Life therapy unless you were over 50, rich or famous. Any younger and you weren't considered worth the business.

No, being young and white was never easy. All you'd have is family.

'Is that why you have no dot,' it suddenly occurred to me, 'because people will make the association with your brother?'

'*No.*' He was clearly disgusted by the notion. 'All I have is *pride* in being related to Billy, and if anyone has a problem with that… I don't even want to *know* them.

'Is it because… *you're* nearing white?' I asked fearfully.

Teddy looked at me, disappointed.

'No,' he said flatly, making me realise at that moment that I had accused him of lying. Accused him of having a scar out of choice, and not by accident. But I couldn't help wonder, having heard the stories about people disgracefully trying to slice off their mortality mole when it showed them the end. 'Would you just stop asking me questions please?'

I pulled my backback up my lap and hugged it. 'Sorry.'

Again, we sat on the rock for a while saying

nothing, watching the water rush as a dense pale wall over the cliff ,only to turn crystal clear into the pool below. I feared in those moments that he would get up and leave, having completely misunderstood me. The last thing I wanted was for this stranger to believe I thought white meant he wasn't worth knowing. That white in his brother meant neither were worth knowing.

'Just so you know,' I said boldly, 'whatever people say, I wasn't put off when I thought that scar of yours was something else. *In fact...*' I went on, indignant, 'I saw that jump you were about to make and I thought *the last thing he should be is broken for the little time he has left*... and your little brother... I worried he'd have trouble getting back to the farm to fetch help for you. So I don't think you're *contagious*,' I said sharply. '*Either* of you. I wouldn't have come back otherwise. *Twice.*'

I caught the side profile of Teddy's face as he turned slightly in my direction.

'So you weren't looking for your friend?' he mumbled.

I hesitated, tempted to tell him she was the last person I wanted to see at that moment, but then said, 'No.'

Teddy's shoulders fell slightly.

'I didn't do the jump in the end. For those very reasons.' He turned and squared with me, intimating something. And the longer I stared at those green eyes, the more certain I became of his meaning. 'I'd surely have broken,' he admitted, making it clear that was precisely what he had *wanted* to happen, to which my eyes widened at the thought. 'And Billy doesn't know his way back,' he confessed. He glanced over his shoulder past me to the high place where he had retrieved his hoodie from, stood there with arms out, contemplating the jump. 'It would have been cruel. All for a moment's frustration.'

I looked to my right, up to the ferned spot and appreciated the height more so now. And that frustration... I could see it too, way up there... looking down on that head of white hair, floating in this deep pool, so far away.

'But you encouraged *us* to jump,' it occurred to me, seeing that the place where Char and I had spied— directly opposite the ferny outcrop—was just as high.

'I don't know.... I had second thoughts when I realised someone was watching me.' He faced the falls, fiddling with his fingers. 'I knew it was stupid. ...I don't know. Maybe I thought if *you* did it... it wasn't that stupid.' He looked pointedly over his shoulder at me. 'Of course, the two of you ran off... so I had to climb down.'

I couldn't tell if he was accusing or grateful until he looked from me to that precarious perch again.

'After you left,' he said thoughtfully, 'I realised I wasn't alone up there. You hadn't been the only ones watching. Billy was. He was down there hooting and hollering, encouraging me... unaware of what might happen... and for some reason, all that escaped me while I was climbing.' Teddy pressed his curled knuckles together like an ashamed little child. 'The last thing I intended to do in that moment was forget about him.'

Chapter Eleven

Invite

'Oh my god! Ivy what are you *doing*?'
Teddy and I both looked up to the top of the falls where Charlotte stood with her fists on her hips, glaring down at us.

'Your mum thought you were with *me*…!' she shouted.

'Yeah well… I'm not,' I yelled back, indignant, '… just like you weren't with *your mum* when you left me to go off with *Jack* again yesterday!'

Her face drew in like a sphincter.

'Well I think your mum would love to know who you've *actually* been with—*what* you've actually been with—don't you?' she threatened, eyeing Teddy reproachfully.

'As *yours* would,' I countered, caring very little what she told Mum.

Just then, Teddy stood up on the rock, grabbed his

towel and hoody and hopped down to the path towards the beach.

'You don't have to go…' I urged, throwing a look at Char that made her storm off. 'Seriously Teddy, don't go.' Hurrying after him, I could see that he wished he hadn't spoken to me about his brother. Himself. '*Please*.... wait...!'

'I shouldn't have encouraged you to come here,' he said resolutely, shaking his head as he stepped over tide pools, to which I kept finding myself in the middle of in an effort to keep up. 'If they find out back at the farm…' he threw me a despairing look '...that I was meeting with a local....'

'They *won't* find out,' I asserted as we came onto the beach. 'You don't need to worry about Charlotte, she knows she'd get in trouble if I tell her mum she's been with Jack. The boy in the red cap,' I explained. '*Really* Teddy—she won't make a fuss of this because she *knows* it'll backfire….' However, I could see my words weren't alleviating any of his fears. 'I mean she makes these sorts of threats *all the time*,' I said more desperately, 'but *she* goes off with people she knows she shouldn't….'

Teddy stopped just then beside the rising tide and stared at me hard. Only then did I hear what I had said.

'I didn't mean it like *that*,' I tried to explain, but he strode off.

'You two are *friends*…' he insisted as I chased him. 'I can't afford to interefere—none of us can,' he nodded towards the farm, miles out of sight. 'We *need* the work….'

'Teddy *listen*.' I stopped him by the shoulder. 'Charlotte and I fall out all the time. I don't even know why I'm friends with her,' I declared, rolling my eyes. 'She ditches me at every opportunity and only comes to find me when someone *else* has ditched *her*. She's *never* really been *a friend*. And she certainly isn't one now.'

With his jaw set, he blinked slowly, wearily, then said in complete disappointment,

'I was afraid of that.' All of a sudden, he turned and headed brusquely for the path up to the dunes. 'If your're not friends' he yelled over his shoulder as I hurried after him, 'there's no need for either of you to be kind then, is there?'

The words stopped me in my tracks, for I spotted at that very moment Char's tall and slim figure stomping to the far left across the field below the golf course, bent on destroying me. *Us.* Seething, I knew I could never again be kind to *that.*

When I checked to see where Teddy had gone, I couldn't find him anywhere. He had hiked up the sand bank and disappeared along the path behind the dunes so swiftly that I lost sight of him completely. It was only when I got up to the golf-course well after both of them that I saw him in his faded green hoody three fields over, heading straight for the hedge at the style. There's no way I could catch up to him, and I hated Char for it.

'You owe me an apology,' Char announced from the bottom of my front steps.

'I don't owe you anything. Now get out of the way. *You* lied to me—again—*I* just didn't fancy telling you where I was going—there's a difference.' I nudged her out of the way easily, leaving her to stand there looking hurt and shocked outside the gate as it swung closed. 'Go away Charlotte. Go find Jack or something.'

'I *can't,*' she spat. 'He's gone white, and Mum won't

let me see him at all now....'

Another of his pranks....

I opened the door, put one foot inside and looked at her pitifully for believing such rot. 'I'm sure you'll find in a week that it was nothing of the sort.'

'*Seriously Ivy,*' she pleaded as I turned from her, 'it's all over the village—all over town. I woke your Mum to find out where you were *to tell you.*' Here, I threw her a doubtful look as she earnestly pressed herself against the gate. 'He's *properly* gone white Ivy' she hastened. 'He was hiding 3...4...5 in school the last few years with tint! And that stunt he pulled on us at the hill... he was trying to see what we'd do if we knew. None of us his age believe it—except me of course—but speak to an adult... speak to my Mum... everyone at the Ward gets notified who's white. I'm not joking Ivy... ask her... *call* her....'

I looked over my shoulder expecting to see the same defiant and desperately selfish expression that was so terrible at convincing me of anything, but this time, and most certainly for the first time ever in our prickly friendship, Charlotte was deadly serious, and holding her phone out to me.

My shoulders fell, reluctant to believe her so easily now.

'And how did you find this out?'

'Well he showed me last night.'

'Where?'

'I met him at the bench on the hill, after I left you at Madame Laurent's,' she admitted, allowing her distress to override her shame. 'He texted me that his mum just found out, that he told her and she was waiting till his dad got home.'

'So this all came from *him,*' I reasoned plainly. 'So

then who else can confirm it?'

'*Ivy…*' Char said incredulously, 'it's on social media.' She knew I didn't have any accounts. 'He's been to the clinic in town first thing and they've confirmed it—his mum and dad have confirmed it on their pages. The Good-bye Celebration is *tonight.*'

Still reluctant to believe any of it, because I only saw Jack's glossy olive-black dot days ago, I quickly got Gran's phone out of the backpack and swiped. It took a few seconds, but she was right. Mr and Mrs Fenner had the invite up on their page. I thought at first it too could be a prank, Jack's against his parents, but I read on. The event was going to be at the school gym and everyone from school who hadn't gone off on holiday yet was invited. Even the Head Teacher, offering the use of the gym in an earlier post, said Jack was the first pupil in the secondary school to go white in the last 25 years.

Jack's news is a shock to everyone. All his peers would want to be there at the Good-bye Celebration the headmaster wrote.

Only it wasn't true—Jack being white *was* a shock—that part was, but the bit about all his peers wanting to be there… well that was a gross assumption. Even if most *wanted* to attend, there would be parents who most certainly *wouldn't* want their children attending. But as I reread the posts, I got the impression that perhaps that's what Mr Goddridge was trying to undermine. That in this unique situation, where no one had the chance to see Jack's dot for what it was, maybe he was trying to get them to see that it didn't actually matter. Jack was Jack, and he was going to die. *Soon.* Any day now, in fact, and he needed to say his good-byes.

Just then, I felt a sickening slither in my middle.

I suddenly realised how cruel I had been to my classmate… much crueller than he had ever been to me. Calling him a liar when he dared to present me with the truth there up at the bench….

'I'm so sorry Char,' I said, tearing my eyes from the comments scrolling in my palm to her genuinely grieved face. 'I had no idea….'

She looked utterly relieved that I finally believed her.

'He talked about hiding it yesterday… just waiting for it to happen without telling anyone,' she explained soberly, 'but I told him what if it happened when he was alone? I told him it was unkind to his parents… his friends…. People *want* to say good-bye. People want to know how long they have with you I told him.' Her lower lip began to quiver and her eyes welled up there the other side of the gate. 'They don't want to assume there's time when there isn't….'

'No, they don't,' I agreed, softening to her. 'Listen Char, you can come in if you want,' I offered, taking the three steps down to her. I pulled the gate towards me and put my arm up around her shoulders. 'I had no idea when you came to find me earlier this was why.' She shuffled slowly up the steps, crying freely now. 'I was horrible to you earlier…. I'm really sorry. What happened back there, none of it matters now….'

Chapter Twelve

Smooth

'When he told you, what did you say?'

'Well I was shocked, wasn't I? I didn't want to believe him,' Char recounted, biting the inside of her mouth, wringing her hands. 'But the more desperate he was that I believed him… well the more I realised he couldn't be lying. There was no reason for him to lie with just me there. So then I was angry.' She stopped herself and looked at me with a crazed sort of expression. 'I was so angry at that point, I told him…' she avoided my eyes just then, making me wonder what she could have possibly said, 'I told him… I wanted to *murder* something.'

I gasped slightly.

'I meant it Ivy.' She squared with me. 'I *meant* those words. I never thought I could say them and mean them, but I did then.' Her focus slackened. '*I* wanted to control death for a change.'

I had no choice but to believe her. Neither of us would

ever use that expression, even in jest. No one would. Only the foulest of people would let such a thing slip off their tongues without thinking, and if it was overheard spoken in a hushed tone to a single ear as it ought to have been, there was nothing to be done but excuse that person for being so desperate to say such words in the first place. Because wanting to *murder* something… wanting to control what *couldn't* be controlled… well it was demanding what could never be done—should never be done. With all of humanity incapable of ending itself, leaving arbitrary death to fall only on plants and animals, insects and such… well murdering… *wanting* to murder… it was perversity and waywardness that could never be.

'What did he say when you said that?' I asked in earnest.

'Well he told me everything at that point. All the tints, how long he had been doing them for… when he left *Grey* and started *White*….' She shook her head slightly, clearly overwhelmed by the things Jack had kept from her. 'And he told me that in Year 7 when he asked me to the disco, that's when he figured out he wouldn't make it past Secondary.'

'Figured it out? How?'

'He went to one of those anonymous charity appointments at the clinic and got a prediction.'

As my eyes widened, I tried seeing Jack walking up to the front door of the clinic at the age of 12, but it seemed impossible.

'And he just *went* in?'

Char nodded. 'He pretended he was delivering newspapers and magazines for the waiting room. Tons of people saw him he said, but no one suspected a thing. Apparently, Mr Goddridge was even there, waiting.'

'Jack saw the headmaster? Did *he* say anything?'
But Char just shook her head. 'Maybe he was more
embarrassed seeing Jack than the other way round,' I
reckoned.

'Maybe,' she shrugged. 'It doesn't change the fact
though that Jack's going.'

'No,' I agreed thoughtfully.

'He's going to be gone Ivy,' she said incredulously,
wide-eyed, like she was only just realising it for the
first time. 'Gone. We'll never see him again.' After a
moment, she rubbed her forehead and said soberly, 'I
wish I had treated him differently now. I wish I had
been honest from the beginning.'

Here, I put my hand atop hers from across the square
dining table and said I wished I could have treated him
differently too. Then as I got up and made us a cup of tea,
the conversation turned from regrets about Jack to regrets
about friendship in general. The importance of being
honest. Telling each other everything. It didn't feel like we
were talking about Jack anymore though and instead I was
beginning to feel like she was taking my own words from
a thousand arguments with her and pushing them back in
my direction. Guiltily maybe, I got the impression that it
was all teasing out the fact that I had been at the falls with a
Transient and hadn't yet volunteered how or why.

'I'm sure there's something everyone wishes they
could do differently,' Char sighed, 'but sometimes you
just can't. And sometimes you can do exactly what you
should have,' she turned in her chair to me, 'and it still
doesn't work out.' I squeezed the teabag against the
inside of Char's mug, feeling immediately her familiar
invitation to row deep in my stomach. 'Whatever you
do, they'll find fault with it. Won't they Ivy?'

There was a heavy silence in the room as I slowly poured the milk and turned with hot mugs to that accusing glare.

'Why wouldn't you believe me when I told you about Jack?' If she could have murdered anyone at that moment, the look on her face made no effort to hide that it would have been me. 'A *real* friend would have believed me,' she accused, setting her jaw.

A *real* friend? Had I *not* believed her? No, a real friend only recognised that after such disappointing news as Jack, Char's first reaction would be to blame the one person she thought she could abuse without consequence. *A real friend* might even let her, considering the circumstances. And a real friend... would stand there until the mugs in her hands went cold accepting whatever trivial injustices she was responsible for as paramount so that Char could walk away absolved of her emotional turmoil.

Like a real friend, the only answer I had this time however was the truth.

'He pranks everyone Charlotte,' I said carefully, bringing the mugs to the table. 'I thought this time was no different.'

'But it was me telling you. *Me. I* don't prank you—so you should have believed me....'

No she didn't prank me. Instead, she lied through her teeth whenever something better came along. Dropped me in the middle of whatever we were doing with no explanation whatsoever to go off and be with people who not once comforted her after their inevitable injuries to her.

'I'm afraid it's because of our track record,' I said, trying not to take or pin blame.

'Jack was *white* Ivy....'

'Yes and you lied to me just before you went off with him,' I reminded her calmly, 'so how am I supposed to just believe everything you tell me when you can't be honest about stuff as stupid as that?' I maintained, unwilling to dance around these facts again.

'Listen,' I sighed, already regretting my forthrightness, 'I know you'll go off and meet whoever whenever you want. And I know you don't always want me around when you do… but I'm not your mother Charlotte. I'm not going to try and stop you… so you could at least be honest—you could at least have respected whatever this is we have by telling me the truth once in a while.'

She was loading up. Of course, her missiles would be that she was misunderstood—that it was my own fault in the first place because I put her in a difficult position—I judged her too much—I obliged her to act and she had no other choice but to lie. She did it to spare me…. Yet again, the whole reason we were here, talking about her lies—trust—instead of grief and loss—wasn't because she couldn't be honest, it was because she felt ashamed. Vulnerable. Yet never vulnerable enough to ask or even accept forgiveness. Never vulnerable enough to show empathy. And now, she was utterly using up all my reserves.

'Char you can't keep doing this—you can't blame me for being careful. What did you expect me to do?'

'He was white Ivy—*white*.'

I rolled my eyes opposite her, aghast.

Surely she wasn't going to hold the fact that I didn't immediately believe her against me. Her lies… his lies… had she been in my shoes she wouldn't have done any differently.

'White,' Char insisted once more.

'Okay fine.' I pushed my mug to the side, resigning. 'He was white... and you told me... but I didn't believe you.'

'No. You didn't. You didn't even believe me when I told you the whole truth Ivy—about his celebration and everything…. You had to go looking on Facebook….'

I wished I hadn't been so flagrantly untrusting now. In fact, I wished I had just shown Char the same kindness I was expecting from her and checked the facts when it wouldn't have been so offensive, because now, I could see that *she couldn't trust me* to trust her.

We were at a stalemate.

It felt as though neither of us could make a move without being destroyed first.

'I'm sorry I didn't believe you Char,' I said simply. 'I should have.' As I watched her that small distance away from me, I saw a vein of indignation pulsing through her, drawing her spine straighter, lifting her thinly-shaped eyebrows and tightening those tiny lips. 'It's a bad habit I've learned,' I accepted. 'Every time I don't believe you, I can see you're left with little choice but to exaggerate or leave a bit of the truth out.' The vein shrivelled slightly. 'And then when I find out what really happened, the cycle happens all over again…. We can't keep doing this….'

'Well then next time believe me,' Char said flatly.

'Okay… I will. But I'll find it much easier if you don't keep stuff from me in the first place.'

I waited for some sort of agreement, to which none came. And as keen as I was to hear her say it, hear her say *I won't lie to you anymore—I won't keep stuff from you*, there was no point in asking her to do here what I was still slightly unwilling to do myself. And that was trust her completely. As much as I wanted our conversation on the matter to end with some sort of unifying promise or voiced intention on both our parts, it ended like all the other times, leaving me feeling like I was dangling off some precipice by my fingers while Char was standing up there with her toes over my knuckles, deciding whether or not to crush them. The thing is, words meant very little when we found ourselves in that predicament. I knew I'd have to prove I trusted her by showing it. And as far as I was concerned, she had no other option but to do the same. Was she going to crush me or not? Did I give her a choice?

'Are you going to Jack's thing tonight?' she asked hopefully, effectively ending our row. 'I know he was never kind to you, but he was kind to me and I can't go.'

'Why can't you go?'

'Mum won't let me.'

'Why? I can't imagine you'd be *alone* with him.'

'He's *White 10* Ivy. You know how people are about it.'

'But she works on the White Wards. That's what she sees *all day*.' The fact that anyone in such a caring profession could be so uncaring to young people out in the community—in her daughter's own school, baffled me. 'Surely she—'

'—She's like everyone else,' Char said plainly, 'and she's set on keeping me in til it's over.'

'But you're going to try and sneak out, aren't you?' I suspected, eyeing her dubiously, feeling lies and lack of trust far behind us now.

'Of course,' Char declared obviously, causing us both to smile. 'What's she gonna do—go there and find me and drag me away?' She grimaced at the thought. 'She wouldn't be caught dead at Jack's celebration.'

The word *caught* us both just then, wiping our smiles from our faces.

Death Dot

Chapter Thirteen

Pasta

Mum sat in front of her plate of pasta, peas and pesto looking a new woman.

'Char came over this morning looking for you,' she said as she pecked fusilli until her fork could hold no more. 'I told her you had planned to go to the falls with her, that maybe you thought the plan was to meet her there. She said she totally forgot about it.' Mum chewed on the pasta and eyed me sideways slightly. 'You two haven't fallen out over it, have you?' I was almost certain she had no idea Char covered for me going to the falls on my own. 'She seemed quite upset.'

Instead of mentioning the falls, I told her what had happened with Jack.

'The Good-bye Celebration's tonight, at the school gym.'

'Oh Ivy...' she wilted, her poised fork almost dropping a dangling spiral of pasta '...that's absolutely awful for the Fenners... their only child....'

I hadn't even thought of that.

'Char said he had been tinting the last few years and that no one seemed to notice. So he went darker and darker, not really checking how fast it was changing underneath.'

'You can get a wash though, to be sure,' Mum said, as if it would have made any difference. 'The White Wards give them out anonymously. Freely. In the post even, if you're too scared to show your face around there.'

'Char said they did that at the clinic this morning. To be honest Mum, I don't think he wanted to know. I think he saw he was lighter than his friends and didn't look back.'

'I'm sure you're right. This is really lovely by the way, dinner. Thank you.'

'It's okay.'

We carried on eating in silence and finished at the same time. When Mum took our plates to the sink, I asked her what she thought of *White 10*. 'I mean, would you have kept me from being near Jack had you known? Char's mum told her she had always suspected Jack of tinting when she found out this morning, and she told Char that was the reason she banned them being around one another. It had nothing to do with his pranks getting in the local paper, or Char being obsessed with spending all her time with him.'

'Ivy, I can't tell you to avoid people nearing white,' Mum said obviously, filling the washing-up bowl with hot water. 'Your old Gran went through it... I'll go through it, and so will you one day. So how is that any different from someone Jack's age? You make your own friends in life Ivy, I can't make them for you,' she insisted over her shoulder as she squeezed soap into the bowl and I gathered the mugs and glasses off the table. 'I mean, it's not like white is contagious or anything' she turned off the tap 'or that hiding it at your age is unheard of.' Grabbing a towel, she then kneaded it as she leaned her backside against the sink. 'Hiding white at your age isn't unheard of Ivy,' she reiterated rather pointedly, 'but it most definitely has its consequences *once people find out.*'

She let the statement settle in the air between us for a moment, making it quite clear as I stood there with fingertips gripping ceramic and glass that people always found out. How could they not? Death of course didn't lie. *White* didn't lie.

'Now I know Jack was a prankster,' she accepted dismissively, 'and I know people have long suspected him of taking from the Transients up at the farm, but let's hope the turnout for him and his family at the school tonight isn't a disappointment, hey?'

After I dropped everything into the sudsy water, I realised what Mum was trying to tell me. Jack would be alienated because of white. If not in Year 7, then now, because even though he was finally telling the truth, no matter what he did, there would always be the likes of Char's mum who tried teaching their children to shun anyone young nearing white. It was no wonder he covered up, if he knew this was how people would treat him. But now he risked rejection from all those he had deceived. Entire sports clubs... teammates... leaders who coached him for years... might never say good-bye to him. The thought of him sitting in that building tonight, seeing only a handful of teenagers who might dare call him a friend... it made me sick.

'I'm going tonight,' I determined aloud, taking a

sponge.

'I think it would mean a lot to him,' Mum encouraged.

'Char's sneaking out to go.'

'Sneaking out? Really?' Mum sniffed at the thought. 'Sara's willing to take away Char's last chance to see that lad?' The thought clearly upset her as she pulled on dish gloves. 'She only has to put up with him for a week. At the most.'

'Maybe she's afraid of what might happen in a week,' I considered, wiping down the table, 'a week where people will be falling over themselves to either avoid him or support him.' It then occurred to me as I shook the sponge over the bin, 'I mean, there might even be people who *don't* care... but want to publicise that fact.' In a small place like Trebullan, it was likely. 'I mean, it's going to get around that a popular teen has been successfully hiding white for years. That's like *newsworthy* after what Mr Goddridge posted— that it's been 25 years since the last white student. So I imagine the last thing Sara will want is one of her family members to be seen publicly associating with Jack. In fact, it would make her more determined if she holds the views she does *and* works for the White Wards.'

I dropped the sponge into the sink and stood beside the fridge, watching as Mum scrubbed and rinsed.

'You know she never liked him in the first place,' I added plainly. 'And to be honest, I didn't either. I mean, it's not like I *hated* him, I just didn't get on with him. I still don't see what Char's seen in him….'

Mum looked upwards out the window to the strip of sky over the road.

'I imagine that's only because you don't know him

Ivy, that's all. I bet he's not hugely different from you or me. The thing is, if he was your brother, no matter how little you liked him, you'd still love him, and the effort to show him empathy would come naturally in a time like this.'

The thought of Jack… practical-joker Jack… as my brother….

'Now I know there's not time to get to know him better,' Mum acknowledged, shoving a fistful of cutlery into the drain basket, 'and I know he's not *actually* your brother… but he obviously meant something to you. So I'm glad you've decided to go tonight, because you'll show him just that.' She was deep in thought now, washing, rinsing, feeling around blindly for what was under the bubbles. 'There's nothing worse than facing the end alone. That's universal. The same for everyone.'

I thought of Gran's texts just then. Her last one.

Mum sighed all of a sudden, disappointed like.

'Unfortunately for Sara,' she breathed, overturning the washing up bowl, 'who spends every day on the White Wards, she seems to have forgotten that fact.'

Chapter Fourteen

Gymnasium

It looked like everyone in our form was already there. Before school finished, Lauren Mills went off to Australia with her family, so she wasn't there. And Char would come any minute. But the rest came. Even the local press.

I arrived to see the headmaster speaking on the patch of grass near the entrance gates to a pencil-skirted reporter and camera man. He gave condolences not just to Jack's family, but to all families facing white as students passed him and headed straight through the tennis courts to the gymnasium.

'Mr Goddridge, taking into consideration the turnout today,' the reporter moved a bit closer to him, readying to thrust the microphone into his face, 'would you say the stigma attached to white is what compelled your student to hide the true colour of his mortality mole?'

Here, Mr Goddridge scratched a sideburn and swelled his cheeks, uncertain how to answer.

'What would you say to those who try and hide their true colour?' the middle-aged reporter pressed, unaware that her own unnaturally black mole stood out suddenly as she lifted the mic another inch towards the headmaster's chin.

'Listen, Jack's a clever, likable lad,' Mr Goddridge defended, teetering on his heels, pushing the woman away slightly with his round belly. 'He has lots of friends. The people you see here have come because of who he is—who he is *to them*. I won't be commenting on the colour of mortality moles. I need to be heading back in now.'

The woman looked around for someone else to interview, but adults seemed to be going out of their way to avoid her as they entered the school grounds.

'You! Would *you* like to tell the Trebullan-Trello-Trep Tri-Area your views?'

'Me?' I looked around, not realising I had moved directly behind the cameraman in order to hear Mr Goddridge's statement.

'Yes you!'

'Uh… um… well… what is there to say?'

She tottered over the grass in her high heels and bent down a bit towards me like she was persuading a young child. I tucked my chin in, wary.

'Did you know Jack Fenner?' She jerked that hideous thing in my face.

'You mean do I *know* Jack? He may be white, but he's still around' I pointed out, apparently annoying her with this fact. 'Yes I know him,' I resigned. 'Unfortunately, I didn't know he was white until today.'

'Unfortunately. Why do you say unfortunately?' The

eager look on her thickly made-up face turned my stomach.

'Unfortunately... because I wish Jack didn't feel like he had to hide his progression through *Grey* and *White*,' I said obviously. 'Because I wish he could make friends like everyone else and not be so concerned about appearing *Black*.' I couldn't help recoil slightly at her own synthetically darkened mole as she pushed the microphone right up to my lips. 'I say unfortunately I only found out because maybe if the media didn't make white at my age so disgusting, then we wouldn't feel the need to hide our true colour and die so alone.'

The woman looked like she smelled dog poo on me and swiftly took the mic away.

'Thank you,' she said curtly, her smile leaching disapproval. 'There's something there we can use,' she then said more to her sidekick than was making any assurances to me. I didn't care though. I wanted to see Jack.

I didn't think someone like Jack... sporty... popular... too cool to be class clown, but just as funny... would even care whether someone like me turned up, but as he sat behind that little table full of letters and cards, receiving the last of a queue of people, he got up and came round and hugged me when it was my turn. I'd never seen him so humble. So sober. It was a Jack I thought I'd always wanted to see... serious for once... only I realised just then that I didn't actually want to see him like that. 16. And white.

Part of me wanted to believe it was all one of his pranks. Part of me hated myself for even thinking such a thing.

'I was never kind to you Ivy... and I'm really sorry for that,' he gushed into my ear, crumpling over me, reducing me immediately to tears.

'It doesn't matter now Jack...'

'It does,' his chin quivered as he tried not to cry. 'You and Char... up on the bench the other day... I knew I could tell both of you....'

'...Until I called you a liar...' I sobbed into his shoulder, prompting him to step back from me and hold my shoulders at arm's length. 'You might have told us Jack if it weren't for me. I'm so sorry....'

'Listen Ivy, the only reason I've told *anyone* is because of you,' he insisted, wiping his eye with the heel of his palm. 'You asked me if there was more to me than lies. Everyone already saw me as a prankster... someone who enjoyed deceiving people... I didn't then want to be remembered as a liar.' He shook his head, convinced, 'I'd much rather have faced white alone.' He then looked gratefully around the room at his team kicking around a football under the basketball hoop by the wall... his form chatting and mulling around the buffet table... the other house captains sitting on the bleachers with drinks, nodding to him as he looked in their direction... and Megan Statt in the corner sobbing her eyes out, unable to do anything about fancying Jack now. 'But I'm not alone, am I?' he posed, appreciating the faces there.

I didn't have the heart to tell him that it was probably because he lied in the first place that everyone came. And I didn't have the heart to tell him that the people in this room never saw his progression from *Grey 1* through *White 10* the last ten years to allow it to slowly shape their minds otherwise. Because not once did they see Jack left out because of the true colour of his dot. Not once did they see a teacher tell Jack that despite his athletic talent, he couldn't be on the team.

There had been no precipitating incident, no adult telling him he might never win, might never be a team captain, determining his entire school sports career. His entire social acceptability. And because no one set that example and paved the way for others to treat Jack likewise, he wasn't intuitively shunned for being literally tainted goods… picked last for the team… left to attend solo at couples' events, or not at all, perpetuating the stigma of white across the sexes. Across all social and academic spheres.

Across the country.

'No Jack, you're not alone,' I told him.

Chapter Fifteen

Billy

'I wish you were *white!*' Char screamed at her mother the other end of the phone. I then heard a door slam. '...Ivy, I've gotta go. I'm not allowed out—she's taking my phone— she caught me trying to go last night.'

There was banging all of a sudden, Sara presumably trying to get into her daughter's bedroom, and then silence.

With Mum already back from her shift and asleep upstairs, I couldn't bear the thought of sitting around here for the next eight hours making every effort not to wake her. And considering Char's threat at the falls yesterday hadn't been because of my whereabouts, rather, her need to tell someone about Jack, I desperately wanted to assure Teddy that Char seeing us together wasn't going to get either of us into trouble.

I took the beach again, and just as I got around the rocky head, I saw Teddy winding his little brother by the hand around marram grass tufts along the deeply carved path down from Point Tar.

I ran ahead and waited as they zigzagged towards me, curling my hands around my backpack straps, seeing how Billy was so much like Teddy, with the same gait, sunken cheeks... golden brown skin and green eyes. The white hair... the height... it was all that seemed different from where I stood.

'You shouldn't be here with us,' Teddy said under his breath to me as they came onto the beach. He promptly brushed passed, leading his brother by the hand to the mound of rocks piled at the cave entrance that hid the falls behind. 'It's probably best you go find your friend or something, don't you think Ivy?' he forced cheerfully, aware now that his little brother was pulling back slightly and staring most curiously at me, apparently more interested than Teddy in my answer.

'Char and I made up,' I assured, following them. 'When she's angry she says all sorts of rubbish, but she wasn't actually upset at me yesterday. She was upset because she found out Jack' I hesitated, for Billy with his white hair and bright eyes—white dot—was still staring back at me, '... she found out he... well you know, *turned*.' I couldn't say *turned white*.

'So Jack in the red cap then—Jack in the news.'

'That's him.'

I stopped short, having forgotten about the reporter at the front of the school and watched as Teddy and Billy navigated around a rock pool. Teddy then hopped to the top of a flat rock behind his brother and turned to me.

'We saw you too,' he admitted hesitantly. 'Billy and I here saw you last night, didn't we Bill?'

That tiny brown face lit up at the realisation of where he had seen me like a lightbulb, with all that white hair atop those bright eyes and teeth. I suddenly appreciated why the little guy had been looking at me so curiously since they came onto the beach. But just as I understood why Billy had been fixated, it occurred to me that he must have seen the article about Jack's dot turning white.

Young Jack.

White.

Perhaps his family didn't hide it, rather, he was too young to understand.

'You saw me... did I say anything?' I asked as we all fanned out across the smooth-topped slate boulders.

'You did,' Teddy said heftily.

'Really?' I started making my way back towards Teddy just as he allowed his brother to lead us a bit. 'I didn't think they'd use anything I said last night,' I confessed quietly, coming a alongside him.

'Well I liked what you said about it being unfortunate that your friend had to hide his progression. That if the media didn't make it so disgusting—'

'—They *included* that? I can't believe they left that in....'

'I reckon someone in editing doesn't like that reporter much,' Teddy chuckled as he hurried ahead all of a sudden and stepped wide over a gap between the rocks, then lifted his brother over it. Together we climbed atop the last large rock between us and the falls and stood there for a few seconds, taking in the scenery.

From this perspective, coming straight in from the sea, the cave looked more like a deep cleft in the cliff face. The walls leaned inwards higher up, leaving a wide crack to the open sky. Seagulls were flying around up there and their shadows cut through the jagged wedge of sunshine where the falls and pool met, casting large, fleeting dark and beastly shadows over the surface of the pool.

'The look on her face…' Teddy referred amusedly back to the reporter, hopping down from our rock, 'she was not pleased. Go that way Billy… that's it.'

We split directions again and made our way over the last ten meters or so of slate towards the little beach beside the pool.

'She wasn't nice,' I decided as I met them on the sand. 'You could tell she was just waiting for me to say something controversial.'

'Well you certainly did that!' Teddy spread the towels on a flat smooth rock nearby. 'Bill I'm not going in straightaway, I'm gonna watch from here for a bit.' He set his backpack down then clipped his brother's float vest on. 'Now you don't need this because you're an excellent swimmer, aren't you?' he spoke kindly to the child.

'*I am!*' Billy shouted enthusiastically, causing a strange echo about the place that frightened a seabird from a ledge and sent its black form flapping up into the blinding sunshine. 'But my arms and legs do get tired…' he whined quietly, aware suddenly that a stranger was listening. I pretended to be interested in the falls above him.

'They do and that's alright Bill,' Teddy assured quietly, glancing over at me. 'That's what this is for.' He put his hand on his little brother's vested chest.

'So I can swim *all day*!' Billy shouted again, taking no notice of me now.

'*Alright*… no need to deafen me….'

Teddy held his brother's hand and led him knee-deep into the water, laughing as the little boy squealed and splashed with excitement. After a few minutes, they eased apart and Billy began to swim confidently just out of reach.

'Not too cold Bill?'

'Nope!'

Teddy put on his green hoodie and came and sat on a towel.

'You can have Bill's if you want.'

'You sure?' He clearly meant it. 'Thanks,' I said, sitting gingerly beside him, aware of a strange confidence building inside me. I didn't know why I should feel such a thing just then, but sitting next to Teddy… a near stranger who didn't think twice about offering me a towel, didn't think twice about offering a girl who clearly had trouble *keeping up* the space beside him when he no doubt could swim and run hours longer than she ever could… well it was something I hadn't experienced before, this indifference to my apparent physical limitations, despite my black dot. I realised just then that Teddy hadn't actually seen the colour of my mortality mole yet, and had been indifferent to that too.

Feeling the crisp, line-dried terry of their towel beneath my legs, I looked down at my shorts and became convinced there was something more to my building confidence than being offered a seat I didn't deserve. As I then watched Billy frolic, it occurred to me that so much boiled down to *Black* and *White*, and yet Teddy hadn't even *mentioned* my dot. Didn't even ask to look at it hiding beneath the ribbed cuff of my hoody sleeve since we met yesterday. Though it seemed the natural instinct of every 17-year-old to compare their own dot to those around them, with Teddy, there was no comparison. No *need* for comparision. If his own was just a scar… what did mine matter next to it?

The lack of curiosity… the indifference… the

invitation to sit beside Teddy without him throwing even a passive glance at my wrist, meant *Black* and *White* didn't matter. He couldn't tell if I'd outlive him by three shades, or if he'd outlive me. That scar of his meant there was no point even looking.

No point judging.

That's what made me feel so confident all of a sudden, I realised. For the first time in my life, my dot didn't matter.

For the first time too, I didn't know what someone else's was, and I was *glad*.

'How did you know my name is Ivy?' I dared to ask, feeling a faint smile heat across my face. 'In the hedge, you said you already knew what it was.'

'Your friend told me,' Teddy readily answered, shaking off his flip flops. 'The one who turned white.'

His eyes were half on Billy swimming circles in the middle of the pool and half on me frowning at the thought of Jack having any sort of conversation with him, because it was Jack who went up to the farm the last few summers and boasted about hiding Transients' tools, toys and personal belongings. Not to mention set off fireworks and steal what he could carry under his sweatshirt without looking too suspicious on his way back down the hill. Of course, he always went straight to Char's like some affection-desperate cat showing up on the welcome mat with a contemptible rodent in its mouth, obliging her to appreciate his gifts.

'Jack? Jack from the telly last night told you my name?' It occurred to me that Jack probably got a rush out of talking to Teddy, who no doubt would have been one of his victims. Unfortunately, he was like that.

Teddy nodded, then explained,

'He asked me once if I had seen you and your friend, described you and all, and told me your names.'

(As much as I didn't want to think ill of Jack, I couldn't help hear his favourite description of Char and me play in my head just then. *Toothpick and Olive.* And I was pretty sure by the unpalatable look on Teddy's face that Jack said as much, not caring that a Transient might find it just as offensive as Char and I did.)

'*Charlotte and Ivy*, he told me,' Teddy went on. 'I think he was more interested in finding Charlotte though,' he cringed slightly.

'No doubt,' I remarked.

'How was it last night by the way, Jack's Good-bye Celebration?'

As he pulled a drink from his bag, I thought of Jack behind that little table, so sober and my feelings towards him immediately softened.

'It was alright I guess. I don't know what I was expecting. I've only been to one celebration—my Gran's. It was like a birthday party I guess. Only no presents. Just cards. I can't believe he wasn't going to tell anyone though....'

'Tell anyone he'd gone white?'

I affirmed with a nod, remembering what Char told me on the front step about not wanting him to die alone.

'It would have been unkind to his friends and family. They obviously would have found out and felt betrayed' I said, understanding now. 'People *want* to say good-bye. They want to know how long they have with you. They don't want to assume there's time when there isn't.'

Something occurred to me just then.

'How does your family deal with not knowing,' I

lifted my chin in the direction of Teddy's hand resting there on his crossed legs, referring to the scar that was all he had left of his mortality mole. 'Don't they want to know?'

'They can find out if they really want to. The colour of the dot is just an indication of the genes. The DNA,' he shrugged. 'But it's not like they can do much about that though, can they? And who wants to spend tens of thousands of pounds on a test that can't change anything? People only do that if they have the *hundreds of thousands* to actually have the genetic editing procedures afterwards. I mean, the simple tests really are only good for finding same-scale donors, for you know transplants and whatever. And no one wants my organs to reduce pain and brokenness,' he said blandly, making me wish he wasn't a Transient just then, 'now do they?'

'But don't *you* ever wish you could know?' I asked, thinking how reassuring it felt that I was behind Char on the scale after all those times I refused to engage in some of her more reckless behaviour, making the most of the time I had instead of squandering health and ability away like she did, the number of times she spent in hospital… but Teddy only shrugged, indifferent. It wasn't like he could do anything about that now.

Despite the freeing feeling of knowing my dot meant nothing to someone like him, I couldn't change the fact that it meant something to Charlotte. With her, my black death dot gave me clout. Credibility. A different kind of confidence. And it took away the fear that my time might come at any moment. Such a thought made me think of Billy over there, splashing and swimming in the water, white as snow. Had I any siblings, I was certain I'd always want to know where any of us stood on the scale.

'What about Billy though?' I cringed. 'You know his colour, and isn't that why you're doing this,' I looked up at the amazing space around us '....spending this...' I didn't want to say *limited* '... this precious time with him?'

Teddy looked at me confusedly, those luminous green eyes discerning.

'You're suggesting that if he was *Black* or *Grey* I wouldn't?'

'No, I'm just saying that *knowing*... might have an impact on the choices we make.'

'Like what, Ivy? Where to live? Where to go to school? Where to hang out—who to hang out *with*?' He gave me a once-over glance. 'I'm afraid those decisions are *already* made for me, and not because of *this*' he insisted, holding up his scar. '*This*...' he looked at the pale spot imbedded into his biscuit-coloured skin and declared '...this is just one way I can keep ignorant people from judging me. It keeps them from assuming they know everything about me... keeps *me* from worrying about my own mortality... because as far as I'm concerned... my progression is *my* business.'

'I didn't mean to—' I tried to explain, only to find that Teddy had sat bolt upright and was now looking at the middle of the pool.

'Billy! ...*Billy*...!'

Billy's little body floated with arms out, eyes closed, his head leaning back in his fluorescent vest. He appeared to be taking in the ray of sunshine that sparkled across his wet slackened face and drove around him into the pool's darkened depths.

Death Dot

Chapter Sixteen

Farm

No one ever really tells you what happens when death comes.

Gran kept saying in her last week that she'd just nod off and it would be done. Death would come and she wouldn't be the wiser. Perhaps somewhere in the back of my mind—in everyone's maybe, there's that assumption that one night, you'd just go to sleep and that would be that. But of course, that wasn't how it worked every time. Sometimes death woke you. Sometimes... you were already awake. The texts Gran left on my phone... her knowing she was about to go... and writing to Mum in the distress of it all... and now Billy there, limp in his brother's arms.... I had no idea death could be so cruel.

'Ivy *help* me!'

I was already up to my thighs reaching.

'Take his legs!'

I did as Teddy instructed and pulled Billy's feet to the shallow edge of the pool where we both lifted him out of the water and onto the thin crescent of a shore.

'*Aaaawh…!*' Teddy let out a guttural cry. 'Oh Bill…' he then said desperately as he fell to his knees and pushed his sopping hair back with two hands, helpless. He searched his brother's angelic face, squaring with death as those little, half-open eyes stared blankly back, unable to focus. 'Billy-boy… *say something*,' Teddy demanded in defiance, then shook his brother's shoulders until those already blue lips parted. '*Please* Bill… *please* not yet… *please not now…*'

But as white glistened through the wet, it was clear to both of us that Billy was gone. Knowing this, Teddy began to sob uncontrollably. He pulled his limp brother up onto his lap and held him tightly in his arms, rocking him back and forth as his mournful cries echoed off the cliff walls and were drowned out by the rush of the waterfall.

I sat in the sand by Billy's slightly wrinkled toes and cried too, not just for his little life gone, but for Gran… and Jack… and Char and Mum. And of course Teddy.

'We need to get him back,' Teddy breathed weakly, sobbing. '…I can't leave him….'

'We can call—' I started for my mobile, thinking help could come to us only for Teddy to remind me there was no signal along the cliffs until the rapeseed field. 'I can help you carry him,' I offered, wiping the tears from my face. But Teddy carried his brother on his own. He closed Billy's eyes, took off his buoyancy vest and strode over the rocks to the beach with his little brother while I followed behind, carrying the bags and towels.

We took the zigzagged path up, and when we got to the top, we passed Melissa and Georgia in bikinis and shorts clearly on the way down to the falls. They stepped out of the way and gave me an amused lingering look as Teddy slipped by with his brother in his arms, still so distressed he was sobbing.

I said nothing to them.

Halfway to the farm, after constant readjustment of his grip, Teddy took a break and leaned against a rock. He wouldn't put Billy down. This time though, when he held his brother close, instead of crying, he seemed to be taking in all the detail of Billy's little body. After a minute or two went by, he kissed his brother's face and started again up the long sandy ditch of a path to the farm with stoic determination.

It took nearly twenty minutes to get to the yard where men and boys were working together moving apples along conveyor belts from trucks to crates.

'*Dad!*' Teddy hollered. The man who turned was the same I had seen in Madame Laurent's. He ran over, clearly suspecting the worst and took Billy, then crumpled to the ground with him in his arms. As engines turned off and machines stopped, I found myself taking steps backwards away from Teddy as a crowd of men grew around him. And when he was whisked away with Billy and his father into the field beside the orchard where the caravans were docked, most likely to tell the rest of the family, I set the backpack and the towels against the open barn door and headed down the farm's main drive out onto Trebullan's north road back home.

Along the high-hedged country road, I feared that was the last time I'd see Teddy. It was unlikely that I'd see him at the falls again. Not after that. There was no doubt he only went because Billy wanted to go in his week of white. No, I wouldn't be seeing him there again, I felt certain.

I suddenly wished I could see him once more, somewhere away from the farm and falls. Realistically, however, there weren't many places the Transients visited outside Churley's orchards and fields anymore. It wasn't like years ago when you were sure to find them at the cove before sunset or the beach between here and Trello when the tide was out on the weekends, fitting in nonchalantly with the holiday makers. Back then, Dad used to make it his business to know where the Transients frequented, and he informed the shopkeepers in the village, the pub and everyone on our street just when to avoid them. But after he and Mum split, no one could bear hearing him kick off about farmhands anymore. Just as well, because in recent years, they kept to themselves. Even visits into town and you could see they only wanted to get in and out; there for necessity only. Teddy's Dad's appearance in Madame Laurent's most certainly wasn't because he wanted ice cream or coffee.

Down the road, I reached midway between the farmhouse and village and came to the style in the hedge where I had first encountered Teddy. Resting my elbows there on its wooden frame, I stared at the spot where I saw his bright green eyes and white teeth. Our short acquaintance and I could see that he had told me the truth. He hadn't looked through the bramble to scare me or spy on me, for there was a trap in there, tripped, with a rabbit noosed and lifeless on the strip of bare earth. I found myself wondering what else he was supposed to do when I had peered in? He did the least offensive thing he could: an uncertain smile with and unassuming *hey*. But of course I ran off like an idiot and assumed the worst.

I suddenly hated my initial distrust of Teddy. Hated how Char and I assumed he was a pervert when really, he was just looking for something to feed his family when I found him there.

I stepped away from the style and wandered down the hill, seawards, unable to get that picture out of my head of Teddy's Dad running to his son in the same way I was sure Mum would run to me if she found me like that. And I couldn't help see those brothers and uncles, cousins and friends gathered around Teddy in the yard, ushering him away to comfort him, because they all knew how horrible it had been for him, carrying Billy like that, all that way. After seeing such fear and compassion up there, I hated the notion that Transients were mean cheats and wicked thieves. I hated too how Dad had put it in my head years ago that they turned white sooner because of it. *Just as well Ivy, they're a wicked, cursed bunch.* And I hated that someone like Billy might be seen as deserving death, or that someone like Teddy only brought grief upon himself. What I saw up at the farm… the same shock and suffering, tears and numbness that death demanded… it was no different from what death demanded of me. And as I thought of the pained look on Teddy's face when he glimpsed that hideous white mark on his brother's lifeless body, I saw nothing different there between us.

I got to my street and spotted Char sitting in front of the house on the bottom step. Though we had smoothed things over yesterday, I was beginning to hate the sight of her waiting there for me.

I got to the gate and expected her to move off the step when the first words out of her mouth were,

'Melissa and Georgia said they saw you with *him* again.'

Her snide, accusing tone undid whatever it was we accomplished yesterday.

'*Him*?' I squared with her. '*His* little brother *died* Char—*while* we were at the falls,' I spat, feeling the heat in my face for having cried most of the way back home grow degrees hotter.

'I think they thought as much,' she accepted with a shrug and scooted over enough to let me past. 'But they said having seen the little boy, they were put off swimming there now probably for the *whole* summer,' she pronounced coldly.

I rolled my eyes, clenched my teeth and got out my key.

'The *whole* summer...?' I mocked.

'Transients didn't know about that place Ivy,' she accused from over her shoulder. 'But now that some haven't just *been* there... but *died* there—'

'—Would you just *shut up!*' I screeched, dropping my keys and spinning around. 'A little boy *just died* Charlotte. Someone's *brother*—someone's *child*.... *You* of all people should be able to show a little compassion!'

'Hey, *I* wasn't the one who made a fuss about it.'

'No, but you're sitting there grilling me like I've been with someone I shouldn't—been somewhere I shouldn't—and *why* shouldn't I? Why shouldn't I have shown an ounce of decency to the only person in this place who actually sees it for what it is—sees people here for who they really are?'

'Get a grip Ivy. He's a Transient.'

I wanted to slap that blazé look right off her.

'Yeah, and your boyfriend is a liar, a thief *and*

a cheat—*to you* and *on you*' I reminded, exploding, unsure of where this well of anger was coming from. 'Yet all *that's* forgotten now isn't it? Why is that Char?' I demanded, crossing my arms. 'Please, tell me? Could it be because he's human and we make mistakes and you're finally getting that... or is it because he's gone white and you just don't want the guilt once he's gone?'

The stunned look on her face could have been any of those answers. All of them probably.

'Death makes us do strange things Charlotte,' I spat '*human* things. None of us down here are any better than that lot up there,' I threw my thumb towards the farm and narrowed in on her, 'but the more we keep thinking how good we are, the worse we become. So I don't want to hear what Melissa and Georgia have to say about their spoilt summer... because they had the chance to do the decent thing and all they did was judge... judge me for helping Teddy and judged him for being a Transient!' I took a step down bending over Char, offending her with my proximity enough that she decided to get up. 'He's human Char,' I bent to her face. '*Human*. Just like you and me. Just like *Jack*.'

She backed away from the steps, eyeing me like she didn't know who I was. But then her expression became measured, threatening.

'Teddy was it?' she took note, staring at me hard. 'Thanks for that.'

I knew that smirk. That horrid little tweak of a muscle just beside the nostril that promised she'd have it in for me. But not me.

Teddy, I realised.

'Get away from my house Charlotte and leave us alone!'

Death Dot

Chapter Seventeen

Photo

All I could think about was Teddy and what she might do to him, what Char might accuse him of doing that would force the entire group to move on. Or worse.

Stories went around these seaside villages about Transients in the past who had been accused of all sorts by the locals only to be forced to leave when there wasn't enough evidence to press charges. And much of the time, they'd leave refusing their pay. *A pseudo-honour or something*, Dad had told me once.

It was no wonder they avoided the locals.

Part of me wanted to warn Teddy about Charlotte, but what good would it have done? No doubt, the second I'd tell him, he'd never want to see me again. If he ever had the chance. And it was possible that Char might not even do anything—that she was just trying to freak me out—and I'd of worried Teddy for nothing. Made him avoid me, for nothing, when he already had enough to worry about.

In any case, I was bursting to tell someone, and with Mum likely to sleep another few hours upstairs, the only other person I trusted enough to keep things quiet was Madame Laurent. I ran to the Plughole, waited in the queue and asked her if I could have a quiet word when she had a minute. As soon as a family cleared out the door with lidded lattes and milkshakes, she beckoned me behind the register into the tiny store room and asked,

'What is it ma chérie?'

'Charlotte.' She didn't know who I was talking about. 'You know, the girl who always comes in here with me. Tall... blonde... thin....'

Madame knew and raised her eyebrows, apparently withholding judgement.

'Yes I know the one, this Charlotte.'

'Well she's angry with me because she saw me hanging out with a Transient. Teddy. She saw me with Teddy.' I felt no shame in saying his name twice. In fact, the more I said it, the more I felt I knew him, was closer to him, like a friend. 'The man who came in here out of the rain yesterday, *his* son,' I explained.

Madame lifted her chin slightly and shifted her eyes worriedly to the left, making the connection.

'Anyway, I was with him again this morning—Teddy—at the falls—and his little brother was there, but then all of a sudden *he died*.'

'—Teddy *died*?' Madame interrupted, apparently shocked as she slumped sideways against the freezer chest.

'No not *Teddy*,' I clarified, finding her reaction to a dying teen—a stranger—albeit a mometary misunderstanding—odd. 'It was his *brother*—Billy.' For a second, she seemed utterly confused, and I guessed that she probably didn't know Teddy was in his teens. It crossed my mind though that perhaps it made no difference to her how old someone was. *White* meant death—grieving loved ones—lives changed permanently.

'So it is *Billy* who died,' she confirmed in earnest, absorbing this fact with a pained look on her face.

'Yes, he was little. Just six. Teddy's 17 and was looking after him in his week of white, bringing him to the falls,' I told her, unsure as to why I felt the need to mention Teddy's age. 'Anyway, they've been going there early each morning this last week and today Billy was playing in the pool beneath the falls… and all of a sudden it happened,' I told her, unable to look at her just then. 'One minute he was splashing around… and the next….'

Madame, who had been eagerly listening and was still leaning against the chest, wilted further into it, clearly appreciating how horrible it must have been not just for me, but for Teddy.

'Anyway, Charlotte's been horrible about it,' I went on. 'She obviously didn't like the thought of me being around a Transient—one that had a white sibling, and so now…' I met Madame's wide, expectant glare '…she and her friends are talking about how they can't go to the falls anymore because a Transient's died there— they're talking about it like some local landmark has been ruined or something.'

Here, Madame checked that no other customers had entered the café then gave herself the liberty of showing real concern.

'So when I got angry about what she and her friends were saying,' I lowered my voice, 'she made out like she's going to *do* something to Teddy. Hurt him or something. After everything he's already going through…. My fear is that she might accuse him of doing something he didn't, and not just hurt *him*, but all of them up there.'

Air had been building up in Madame's cheeks and when I had finished, she finally let a puff of it escape from her lips in complete frustration.

'It is a shame about the little one Billy,' she acknowledged sadly, frowning and swallowing hard, 'and the middle child, Teddy,' she went on, making me realise she knew more about this family than I had told her, for it only occurred to me that Teddy might be a middle child—a middle child whose older sister had collected Billy from the falls that first day—a middle child I hadn't mentioned to Madame, '…Teddy will not escape the stigma,' she assured gravely. 'However, when you say this Charlotte made out like she was going to hurt him, did she give you any indication what she intends to do?'

'No.' Madame's shoulders fell slightly. 'But she's not afraid to lie,' I made quite clear, propelling her into careful thought. 'And she hates that lot up there like everyone else does around here,' I reminded. 'All it takes is a rumour—it doesn't even have to be the truth and people lap it up if that's what they're already believing.'

'Of course you must understand that I am not like everyone else,' Madame quietly assured me as she glanced at the two older ladies over her shoulder who sat at a small table by the window. 'I am but a foreigner here as well,' she insisted through her anglified French accent.

'I know, and I wouldn't have told you if I thought…'

'We are *liked-minded* about...' she stated discreetly, stopping me from saying too much, something that might be overheard. Then surreptitiously, she raised her brow in the direction of the rapeseed field atop the sloping cliff behind the shop, indicating the farm, the Transients. 'You have your associations, I have mine.'

I wasn't quite sure what she meant by that, however I got the distinct impression she was admitting to some sort of connection with the Transients.

'I saw you offer Teddy's Dad a drink yesterday,' I acknowledged as she checked the ladies again. 'You looked disappointed when he refused it.'

'They are afraid to be accepted,' Madame shrugged a shoulder, 'just as those here are afraid to accept them. But with lies about, can either blame the other?' The bells on the shop door rang and she urged me to stay put while she dealt with the customer.

'I think it might be wise to tell Mr Briggs, the farmer,' she reckoned when she came back to me.

'What good would that do?'

'He can keep an eye out for trespassers. Anyone coming onto his land that shouldn't. And I think it's worth telling Antony Harley...'

'The *constable*? Isn't that a bit much? I mean it's not like Charlotte's actually *done* anything yet.'

'Ah but my dear, if we do not tell my good friend about a threat, then what will it look like after, if an accusation is made?' I felt myself shrivel at the thought of going to see Antony and wished I hadn't come to Madame after all. 'It is important to prevent escalation if at all possible ma chérie.'

'Yes but isn't that what *we're* doing by going to the police?' I argued.

'Ivy, Mr Briggs' workers are a vulnerable group of people. Threats to them should not be ignored.'

It hadn't occurred to me that Transients were vulnerable, but of course they were.

'All it takes is an insinuation to keep them from working in these parts again,' she reminded, 'and it will no doubt follow them wherever they work, up and down the country. Mr Briggs finds this particular family his hardest working and would do much to protect their reputation, I can assure you. Why do you think they avoid local businesses and entertainment unless absolutely necessary? Because he has told them what the village is like. Because he is trying to protect them.'

'*The farmer* tells them?' I asked, disheartened that such measures had to be taken. 'But shouldn't they be allowed to come down here and do what everyone else does—do what they like?'

'They should Ivy, but they know they can't. You saw how the gentleman was in here.' She motioned to the door, the rain when Teddy's dad had come in two days ago. 'He was afraid. We all know they cannot be just like everyone else. That is why we must protect them where we can.' She put her hands on my shoulders and squared with me. 'If you allow me, I will speak to Mr Briggs… and I will be sure not to mention Teddy specifically, or this Charlotte you speak of. I will be general if he presses me. Whatever is going to happen, it would be good for us to take advice from our good friend Antony in this situations, no?'

With it all sounding informal and anonymous now, I nodded, feeling like a weight had lifted from me until I got a text and looked at my phone on the pavement outside the shop moments later.

There in a message from Char was a picture of Teddy carrying his brother. It had to be from Melissa or Georgia before we passed them on the top of the cliff. They must have seen Teddy coming and took the picture before we got to them. Char's text below it made my stomach turn:

Could this be the face of a criminal Ivy?

I passed the two older women coming out of the Plughole and went straight back into Madame and showed her, feeling already the damage beginning.

'Please, you have to do something,' I urged as she squinted at the photo.

'What is this?'

'It's *him*—Teddy—with his brother Billy—the one who died.' Panic filled me at the thought of this image being passed onto at least twenty people by now with the way Melissa and Georgia distributed trash. 'This is after he died,' I hastened. 'He's taking him back home there.' I came round to see if I was visible behind Teddy there in the photo. 'See that... my head's down, but that's me with the towels, following him. We passed the girls who took this photo on the path and they're in my year at school. They're the ones who are making a big deal about a Transient dying at the falls. I had no idea...' I started to say, seeing Billy's limp face, that lazy gaze, and the darkness inside his parted lips as Teddy carried him, which somehow took my words and thoughts clean away just then.

Madame appeared to gauge my anxiety, handed me back my phone then went and flipped the *OPEN* sign to *CLOSED* on the shop door.

'...*Face of a criminal*...' she muttered under her breath. 'Ivy we go there now,' she determined grabbing her handbag from under the till. 'No boy is going to be accused today!' she declared, throwing up a finger to the sky. 'Come—we walk.'

We left through the back door of the shop and marched up the hill to Trebullan's little police station that was no bigger than a double garage.

'Antony,' Madame said kindly over the counter to the head of greying hair at the computer, 'we have a delicate matter we'd like to discuss with you urgently.'

The slim, tall man stood up and stretched his broad shoulders back, apparently glad for the interruption.

'Would you like some privacy?' He offered the room to his left, between the single cell and toilet facilities.

'Here is fine,' she dismissed.

Antony propped his weight onto an elbow, appearing quite pleased that he could be of any use to Madame Laurent who was not only attractive, but of similar age and widowed too.

'What is it I can help you with then?' he asked.

'Ivy tell him what you told me,' she urged, still mildly flustered.

So I told him, and showed him the photo.

Afterwards, I felt certain Char and I would never be friends again.

Chapter Eighteen

Empathy

'Well of course they're not going to do anything,' Mum sighed as she came out of the utility room. 'And why didn't you wake me? As much as I love Camille, I don't like the thought of her taking you down to the police station for a statement—even an informal one.'

'He didn't take a statement, Mum. Literally, he logged it like a complaint or something. They can't do anything unless Char actually makes an accusation first.'

Mum laid her uniform over the back of the chair and smoothed it out distractedly.

'Of course, it'll be impossible now to mend things with Charlotte if she finds out.'

'It's always been impossible with her Mum.'

'I'm just saying...' she exhaled, cleary frustrated, then went and filled up the kettle.

'You're just saying what?'

'It's just petty really, all of it, that's all.' She popped the kettle on and crossed her arms, waiting. 'When you think about what's happening with Jack… and now this little lad you mentioned…. I wish people would just show a bit more kindness,' she said as she watched the red light glow at the base. 'Compassion or something.'

'Yeah well so do I Mum.'

'…I mean, part of me wants to tell you that you can't see Teddy anymore… but that's the part that's just worried what people around here will think.' I spun completely round on the chair gauging how serious she was. 'And part of me wants you to be friendly with him just to spite them all… show them how people *should* be treating one another….'

'Yeah well I don't care what anyone else thinks' I said flatly, hanging my elbow over the back of the chair. 'Teddy's kind. He's been nicer to me than any of my friends have *ever* been. All the stuff the others care about—*who's with who*, who thinks they're all that, and *looks* all that—Teddy's not said one word to me about any of that stuff.'

'I'm glad Ivy,' she threw me a pointed look. '*I am*, but you can't allow your relationships around here to fall apart for someone who'll only be here for a season.'

'*I'm not.*' I recoiled, offended at the insinuation. After all, it was Charlotte who made the threat. It was Charlotte who always ditched me until she herself was ditched by someone else. And it was Charlotte who made Melissa and Georgia's photo more sickening than I ever thought she was capable of. 'I'm just keeping my distance from those who enjoy humiliating strangers,' I said obviously. 'Melissa and Georgia and Charlotte… they didn't think twice about taking advantage of

Teddy's situation the second they saw him down,' I said through clenched teeth, recalling that look the girls had given me when we passed them on the cliff. Then as Mum got out a mug and dropped a teabag into it, I pointed out in earnest, 'They *took a picture* while Billy was there in his arms… they *knew* what was going on… and they didn't care. Surely you don't want me hanging around people like *that*.'

'I don't Ivy,' Mum insisted just as the kettle boiled to a stop. 'Don't get me wrong. I don't want you having anything to do with those girls after what was sent to you on that phone,' she made clear, pouring water into a mug. 'You want one?'

'No thanks.'

'What Charlotte put on there was quite disturbing and I'm glad you'll let me have a word with her mother… but I think my point is… you have to go to school with these girls…. *You* will be the one to negotiate avoiding them in the village and town…. You have another few years at least before you all start going off to uni or getting jobs and I'm worried you'll feel like a prisoner in your own home if they rally against you.'

'So what then? What do you expect me to do? Just forget how horrible they all are and act like everything's okay?'

'Ivy, I'm not asking you to do anything. In fact, that's precisely what I'm asking you *not* to do. Burning bridges right now, in the heat of the moment, may very well escalate things. These girls are being this way for a reason.'

'—Because their vile Mum.'

'—Because they're ignorant Ivy. They are so focused on how they think and feel, they don't have the capacity to even consider how others might.'

129

I suddenly realised where she was going with this.

'And the moment I can't empathise with them… *I become like them,*' I mocked slightly, taking Gran's motto for dealing with biased townfolk and seeing suddenly that it unfortunately applied to my own friendships.

I turned around and curled indignantly into myself there at the table as Mum came over and pulled out the chair opposite with her uniform on the back. She didn't say anything. She didn't have to. I had said it for her.

'Your Gran was a wise lady, Ivy. Sometimes I didn't want to hear what she had to say, but as I got older, I realised her way of doing things meant her friends were devoted, her enemies respected her… and she bore no malice, or shame or guilt in any of her relationships.'

I couldn't be too annoyed with Mum for wanting to remind me about empathy. If Gran had been sitting in the room, she'd have no trouble telling me. She said it every time half a story was told. Usually my half. *There is another side to this Ivy,* she'd say, *a side with a human no different from you, experiencing the same range of emotions as you do, deserving the same understanding you come here seeking from me. We're not so different,* she'd tell me.

But when I tried to have an empathetic thought for Charlotte after Mum went to work, I saw that photo of Teddy again and simply hated her for it. The toil on Teddy's face, the grief there… I hated her for mocking him at that moment in his life… Billy's death.

Chapter Nineteen

Jack

Something inside me thought it all wasn't real.

When I had seen Jack at the table there in the gym, I really wanted to believe he was white, but I couldn't help entertain for a split second that maybe it was all an elaborate prank. His best one yet perhaps. Of course, it would take only a week to be proven one way or the other.

It wasn't a week for Jack. He died sometime in the night and I felt awful for having thought white on him showed anything other than the truth.

The hatred I had for Charlotte consequently, though unexpectedly, melted away, even when I looked at the photo she sent me of Teddy and his brother. For some reason, I imagined that when she thought of it, thought of whatever she intended to do with it, she would see the grief there on Teddy's face and somehow understand that he wasn't so unlike her after all, she wasn't so unlike him.

'Do you think you'll text her?' Mum asked when she came in, having heard the news herself about Jack.

'I thought about it,' I admitted, scraping the sides of the bowl with my spoon to gather up the last flakes of cereal, 'but then I thought maybe she'll take it like I was trying to rub her nose in it or something.'

'Rub her nose in the fact that Jack's died? I can't imagine her thinking that right now Ivy.'

'I can.'

Mum stripped off her uniform in the utility room and came out in a plain white t-shirt looking tired as usual. She made us both cups of tea and took my bowl and spoon away to the sink in silence. I could tell she wanted to say something more but didn't quite know how without offending me.

'Just say what you want to say Mum,' I encouraged after she went and sat on the couch and just stared for a moment at the blank telly. 'I know you want me to text… I just don't know what to say.'

'It's not just that Ivy,' she said thoughtfully, turning her mug into her palm. 'Were you close with Jack?'

I wasn't sure where she was going with this. 'No. Not really.'

'And Charlotte was?'

'Yes. They were together. Sort of. But he couldn't stand me, and made that apparent.'

'But he apologised at the gym?' she rested her chin on her shoulder and looked at me from across the room.

'Yeah. He was sorry for how he treated me. He said it was because of me that he told everyone the truth. Because I called him a liar. And he didn't want to be known as a liar when it came down to it I guess.'

Mum turned back to the telly, despite it being turned off and said delicately,

'White makes you realise who you are I think, Ivy. It forces you to consider the things that are important, things you took for granted through black and grey. Jack did a difficult thing, telling everyone, but because he did, people are coming out and showing their real colours all over the country.' She looked at me again, this time pointedly, suggesting Jack's story had been trending or something. 'Young people. Everywhere.'

'Because of Jack?' I found it difficult to believe.

Mum nodded. 'Charlotte's done a tribute page to him this morning, telling his story. She must have done it after midnight, or maybe had it prepared in advance, because the girls pointed it out at work and it wasn't there when we had break at 11.'

I grabbed my phone and quickly flicked. The link was on Charlotte's page. I clicked and found Jack, smirking, set across the banner. Inset photos of friends. One of me and Charlotte. I scrolled down. There, Charlotte described Jack's wicked sense of humour... his difficulty with *Grey*... his athletic and academic successes that helped him to hide it. But then there at the bottom was a photo, a letter Jack had written to her. I zoomed in. The date on it was yesterday.

Charlotte, I tried hiding white and realise now that in doing that, I've only ended up robbing you and my family and friends of the security that I'd be around longer than will be possible. Since Year 8, my conscience has grown heavier. These last few weeks have been the most difficult because every time I saw you Char, I ached at the thought of telling you as much as I ached at the thought of us planning another time to meet like we had all the time in the world. I wanted to say something but couldn't. I kept trying to find ways of convincing myself that you'd accept me white if you knew. But I always chickened out. Then when it came—when it properly came—I was afraid I might go at any moment and leave you and my family in shock. The thought of you finding out after it had happened, I can't bare it even now. You're grief would have been unexpected and cruel, and it would have been all my fault, because I was ashamed. Because being white and 16 makes us too old for people to be kind and too young for them to care. But you've been kind Char. You've always been kind. You still care. I know you couldn't come to the celebration, and I can pretty much guess why, but trust that the reason I can accept who I am without even an ounce of shame—accept white is what I've become, is because you gave me the courage to face everyone else. You accepted me for what I am. The most important thing I wanted this last week was to be able to face you without fearing you'd reject me. I couldn't have asked for a closer friend. I never meant to hurt you Char. I never meant to give you false hope. And I never meant to break your heart with grief.

Remember me on your way to white Char. Remember that everyone faces it. The world will try to cover it up and even judge you if they spot it coming, but there's no shame in being human. There should be no shame in being white.

With Deepest Love
Jack x x x

I hadn't realised tears were running down my cheeks until I had finished. And as I quickly wiped my face and scrolled down a bit more, I began to read what Charlotte wrote in response, that her own mother prevented her from going to Jack's Good-bye Celebration… that white wasn't just acceptable for the aged… and that yes, we were all human and should face it without the same fear of rejection Jack had experienced. *Death was a consequence of being human,* she wrote. *How we treat people shouldn't depend on the colour of their mortality mole.* #DeathDotDecency

Who was this Charlotte? I admired her and loved her. And so did the 332,789 others who had liked what she posted.

'332,000…?' I mumbled incredulously under my breath as I wiped my face again with the back of my hand.

'Oh *that's* gone up since tea break this morning,' Mum noted. She then turned back round to me. 'Ivy I know you weren't close with Jack, and I know you and Char have had a difficult time of it lately… but do you really think she'll take a text from you as rubbing her nose in it?'

'Probably not,' I admitted, scrolling up and seeing Jack's smirk again. 'But it's not that I don't *want* to say anything to her,' I made clear 'because as soon as I found out about Jack this morning I wasn't angry anymore about the picture she sent me. It's just… I don't know… I don't know what to say… or how she'll take it.'

'I'm sure she'll take it the way you intend it, Love.'

'It's just tricky…' I said grudgingly, knowing I needed to send something, and soon.

'Of course it is,' Mum soothed. After a beat, 'What Jack did has broken all the rules,' she said plainly. 'He hid white, then publicised it, and while people have had their Good-bye Celebration for him, they've not really had the years of mental preparation that he'd be going sooner than all of them. That *is* tricky. But Charlotte's broken all the rules here too. And the grief of Jack gone now is hitting the young people in Trebullan hard' she reckoned, nodding to my phone, 'and it's becoming bigger even than our little village now.'

I watched as Mum got up and grabbed her own phone off the mantle then sat back down on the couch.

'Charlotte's just shown here how unkind society is on our young when they turn white,' she said, swiping, presumably scrolling the comments on the site, '...the measures Jack had to take... all because he wanted to enjoy his short life.' After a moment, turned off her phone as though a bit overwhelmed by it all. What I was feeling, no doubt. 'We're all guilty of it though. Discrimination' she acknowledged distractedly to the empty screen. 'So how do we deal with it?'

I looked back down at Char's page devoted to Jack and couldn't help think of his last words to me.

...People already saw me as a prankster, I didn't then want to be remembered as a liar.... I'd much rather have faced white alone. I saw that grateful expression as he looked around at his friends and family in the gym. *But I'm not alone, am I?*

He absolutely wasn't.

'We deal with it together I guess,' I determined, clicking *Like.*

Chapter Twenty

Char

Char's post of Jack's nearly unexpected death on the internet was gaining momentum. The 332,000 the hour before had become 500,000 as people around the country started waking up and sharing it around the world. Every time I refreshed the page, another few hundred appeared and the comments were rolling in. They mentioned the culture of tinting, of hating the need to hide, and of fearing no one would fancy them if their true colour was on display. Then there were the praises... the comforting words about Jack and has bravery, then the experiences. Username after username popped up with how they knew someone who had been badly treated through grey and white and ended up alone in their last week.

How is it that children are forgiven for turning white but the world holds it against us the second our armpits start to smell or our faces come out in spots? one person wrote.

Another,

Why don't we deserve a first love at the age of 16, or a family at 23? What is it about 13-30 that makes people wary of us? Grey? White? If anything, we know what we want and won't mess anyone about.

But there was another type of comment starting too. Those who clearly had no idea what it was like to been a teen turning white,

What a selfish lot you are, expecting partners and children to just get on without you! Have you no concern for the broken hearts you'd leave behind? Have you any idea how unfair that would be to them?

Of course, like seagulls descending on a dead fish rolling in off the surf, scores of responses followed, picking and tearing apart such nonsense.

Whatever Charlotte had started here, it was as if the country had been waiting for it. The shame in hiding white... the shame of dying unexpectedly and leaving loved ones behind with no knowledge... it seemed the majority of comments confirmed that no one really ever had the nerve to carry on hiding in their final week. In fact, all the related posts I could find said that when white truly came, they had to confess, partly because legitimate parlours refused such cover-ups, and partly because the home-brewed alternatives were done badly, arousing suspicion even for the most determined. And some even mentioned that the mind went through something then. An altruistic resolution. *It just isn't worth it. It isn't worth pretending if it meant your closest and dearest were so unaware that you might potentially die alone in your last week.* And as I scrolled through the comments, some wrote that they had personally seen loved ones lie, confessing right before the end, just like Jack.

I carried on reading, finding that a fair number of posts explained how the stories of deceased brother's and sister's were hushed up to benefit the family—the unfortunate genetics that decided an early mortality were concealed, improving the chances of social acceptance for their siblings.

I think my mum was glad Adam tried for so long to keep it quiet, KLAYRE__BEAR posted in the thread. *We moved away, she told me not to talk about him or else everything he did for me would have been in vain. She never mentioned his name again and this is the first time I have since he went white 10 years ago. Of course, ADAM didn't go through all that effort to hide for ME. I wasn't even born when he started tinting. He faked black to hide from our mum and everyone else who thinks like her!*

I couldn't read anymore, yet I was so proud of what Charlotte had started here.

Turning my face up to the blinding blue sky, the sea, I squinted and sighed further back into the bench above the golf course and contemplated against the roaring wind what I should text to Char. After another read of Jack's letter and her post beneath it, I wrote something simple and honest.

I miss Jack. And I miss you.

Her reply was quick.

I miss you too Ivy. Please let's not fight.

And within minutes, we were texting sorry's that felt more genuine than all the others we had ever said to each other's faces in the past.

Where are you?

Churley's rapeseed.

From my elevated position beside the dunes,

I looked across the golf course and fields to see if I could spot her, but the contours of the landscape left a stubborn hump blocking the blanket of yellow I knew to be just beyond. I texted her where I was and invited her to come to the bench with me.

Then there along the seam of two fields I saw the top of Charlotte's slender frame easing up the path and coming into full view. She waved and so did I. They weren't fervent waves. Just a hand up, then down. Solemn waves across a long distance.

I didn't wait for her to cross two more fields and clamber up the sandy hill beneath me. Instead, I ran to the path at the bottom of the golf course and met her halfway, wrapping my arms around her the second I recognised her eyes were bloodshot and puffy.

Chapter Twenty-One

Track

The last time we both were there we had called him a liar. But Char reminded me that because of it, Jack came clean about his shade.

'He wanted me to tell you it was the turning point for him,' she said as we stared at the rocky island a mile or so out that only birds inhabited. 'He said he came up here to show me and then lost his nerve, but it was what you said about there being more to him than lies that changed his mind in the end.' Char looked at me as Jack had, grateful that I had said such an awful thing.

'He told me in the gym,' I confessed, still feeling guilty for wanting to believe he had lied when he had clearly told the truth. 'I saw your post that you didn't get to see him at all. I thought you might have made it there after everyone else left, or snuck to his house or something.'

'No, my mum locked the front door and windows

and turned off the wi-fi. She said I could *text* good-bye.'

It sounded exactly like something her mother would do, and having heard their row on the phone the morning after Jack's celebration (just before I went off and found Teddy and his brother), the disgusted look on Char's face no doubt told only the half of it.

'She's regretting it now though,' Char said darkly. 'She forgot I can get good signal up in my room, and when I saw Jack's mum posted an update about him in the night, well I had to do something, didn't I?' She blinked upwards, holding back tears. 'Her friends saw what I put up and told her she shouldn't have been so stupid keeping me from seeing Jack. They've put the fear in her now that all the youth in the Tri-Area are gonna try and break anyone with her views.'

'Seriously?'

'How do you think I got out of the house this morning?'

I looked Char's spent frame up and down, assuming she climbed out of a window and snuck out like she usually did. But there wasn't the mischievous air about her this time.

'So she just *let* you out?'

Char nodded, stone-faced.

'What, she thought you'd try and put her in *hospital* if she tried keeping you?' I imagined ridiculously.

'I think she believes I control the masses right now,' Char said dismissively, distractedly. 'Thinks young and white have nothing to lose and everything to gain by making examples of people like her.'

'But that's absurd. Who would waste their last weeks vengefully breaking *anyone* like her?'

'No one Ivy. But that's what they're afraid of.

Because they see us as some sort of threat. But if it makes them think twice about locking those of us who aren't even white in houses... or keeping any of us from having relationships, then I don't care if they believe we're out to steal time from them living their lives they're quite happy to steal off us.'

I could see it just then, heart attacks and anxiety, people filling Accident and Emergency with all sorts... blaming it on the young and *white*... fuelling fear. ...None of it true.

'They want to be the victim right now,' I declared. 'How else will they be able to justify their prejudice against us in the first place?' But my point fell on deaf ears, for Char was caught up in the distance with a pained look on her face.

'You know what she said to me this morning?' Her expression was fixed, and I could see her drawing something from there, wherever there was, and dragging it here to the bench. 'She came up, thanked me for the hundreds of trolls she was getting and said the wi-fi was back on, and then *Oh, Jack died in the night, in case you wanted to know.* Like he was nothing. He was *something* when she got to work though.' Char swallowed hard and let the tears stream down her now blank face as that thing in the distance seemed to disintegrate.

'Ugh Char... I'm so sorry ....' I put my arm around her and leaned my head onto her shoulder, but in the wanting to comfort her, I could feel something rigid there holding me at a distance. To me, it seemed like resolve. With no way to bring Jack back and no way of saying good-bye to him properly, it became apparent that Char was now set on a path that needed her to remain wounded. Required her to be. Until those like her mother changed the way they thought of people like Jack, there couldn't be any comfort.

'Listen Ivy... I was just wondering if I could be here by myself....'

I looked thoughtfully at her, realising that she had been on her way here before I'd even asked where she was.

'Of course.'

I got up, pursed a smile and cut over the top of the dunes, feeling like everything had changed all of a sudden. It seemed only last month white didn't really mean anything, but now... it was everywhere. Death was everywhere. And if it wasn't *White* and Good-bye Celebration invites, then it was *Black*, on the telly... in magazines... brutally flaunting its gift of time.

That, or faking it.

No, everything had changed in a month. Had I known before how afraid Gran would have been in her bedroom, facing it alone... I wouldn't have left her. I wouldn't have been so foolish to hope I could wake up before death. And had I considered the real predicament of others my age who were white... I might not have doubted Jack even when I saw him for the last time in the gym.

Guilt seeped its way through me just then, and it began to drip from my eyes in hot spike-like tears. Before I even realised I was walking along the dirt track across Churley's Farm, I heard the shriek of a child and thought instantly of Billy. Billy scaring that bird up into the sky. Then I thought of Teddy carrying him to the yard. The yard maybe a hundred metres beyond the hedge to my right, behind the farmhouse.

Melissa and Georgia, throwing that awful look at me, stung deep into my eyes, making me wish I had done something, *said* something, kept them from taking that photo.

The faster I walked, the more I cried.

'Ivy!'

Involuntarily, I turned and looked, but ashamed, I pretended I didn't hear or see.

'Ivy *wait!*'

The quick crunch of feet jogging towards me from behind made me panic and I too began to run.

'Ivy *please....*'

I don't know what I was thinking, running like that, but Teddy's hand on my shoulder as he caught up with me was what really stopped me; that gentle touch from someone who might possibly understand what it was like to find death suddenly everywhere, changing everything inside you before you even had the chance to make sense of it all.

'I'm sorry....' I blurted, looking down at the track, the dust still settling between our feet '...I just... I didn't...' I didn't know what to say, or how to say it. All I could think about was Billy in his arms... Jack behind that table... and Gran like an angel in the morning light, after the bird's shadow crossed her face. I avoided Teddy's eyes as my chin tightened and lip began to quiver, but no matter how hard I tried to stop it, I couldn't help but sob.

'It's okay...' Teddy soothed, his voice already cracking, '...it's okay....'

Without a word, he put his arms around me and let my tears dilute the cherry stains on his t-shirt.

When I had calmed enough to hear his heart beat a dozen times or so, I took a step back and saw that his face could be no less red and puffy and grief-stricken as mine.

Death Dot

Chapter Twenty-Two

Relief

'I saw you from the orchard on the dunes.'

He looked hopeful slightly, checking that I didn't mind.

'I'm glad,' I confessed, though found it difficult to tell him to his face.

Then as I fiddled with the hem of my top, I had the sudden irrational fear that he knew I had spoken to the police, knew of Melissa and Georgia's appalling photo.

'You know I'm not ashamed that I know you Teddy,' I found myself declaring. 'I mean, it makes no difference to me you're a Transient.' I didn't mean to glimpse his scar just then. 'And it doesn't matter what colour you are either,' I insisted, covering myself. 'In fact, I wish *I* had the privilege of not knowing,' I began to talk rubbish, nodding to his hand, only to regret what was coming out of my mouth instantly. 'I mean...' my eyes rolled, loathing '...what I'm trying to say...' I sighed '...is that all

I can think about right now is *White*... and *Black*. And...'
I caught his eye and diverted back to fiddling with the
edge of my top '...death...' I said under my breath.

Teddy swallowed hard, but said nothing. It was okay
though, because I knew we were thinking the same thing.

A loud clatter rolled through the air just then.
It sounded like a tower of palates had toppled in the
nearest yard up at the farm. Teddy looked only slightly
concerned by the noise, like he knew what it was but
didn't want to have anything to do with it.

'Do you have to get back?' I asked, his eyes looking
in the general direction of the barn and outbuildings.
The last thing I wanted just then was for him to leave.

'No. They've got me as a floater today.' He looked
down at the fresh cherry on his shirt, presenting it as
some kind of proof. 'Packing. They've got plenty of
packers up there.'

'They had you working today?' It was just like Mum,
back at her shift despite Gran's bench not even in place.

'Well what else was I going to do Ivy?'

'I don't know.... I don't know what anyone's
supposed to do,' I shrugged. 'It just feels like the
world should stop though, like it should take time to
understand what's gone missing from it...' I determined
boldly, meaning not just Billy, but Jack too. *Gran.*

'Well something in me stopped,' Teddy said.
'Something in all of us did up there.' He lifted his chin
towards the hedge. 'Whether or not the world outside us
recognises anything, I do—*we* do—and that's what matters.'

My eyes fell from his and down to the watery
cherry stain.

'It just feels like we try to forget them too easily,'
I said, understanding that this was why I hated Gran's

bed being gone. 'It feels like betrayal.' I looked up at Teddy in earnest, 'It feels like the world never really tries to accept what happens and instead just covers it up.'

He looked away like my words had been offensive.

'Ivy, we spend our whole lives accepting what will come.' From the minute we were born, someone was there comparing our shift until we started doing it for ourselves. Please don't say the world doesn't try to accept what's coming.' He turned those puffy, red eyes on me again. 'Do you know how many *months* I saw white on my brother and had to accept it? I didn't have *a choice*—I couldn't *look away...* it was there, every minute of every day, reminding me, *reminding all of us*' he said almost angrily now. 'So just because I don't have to fear what's coming anymore, because it's already happened, and I've gone back to work, doesn't mean I'm trying to cover up the loss of a brother' he declared sharply.

'I didn't mean it like that.'

We were both quiet for a moment after that and I could see as I used my sleeve to wipe my eyes that my apprehension, my silence, had brought a defeated sort of expression over Teddy, like he was frustrated with himself for having been so abrupt.

'Listen,' he said finally, 'I wasn't looking out for you so I could upset you. The whole reason I chased after you was so I could say *thank you*. That's all. Thank you Ivy for helping me back after...' it seemed he was trying to find different words, then thought better of it '... after Billy died. You didn't have to follow me... or wait with me when I had to stop, and you didn't have to come all that way. You didn't have to do any of that, but I'm really grateful you did.'

'It's okay.'

There was something more he wanted to say.

'Listen, I wanted to tell you….'

He hesitated and started again.

'You asked me before about this,' he held out his wrist all of a sudden, 'about it being an accident.' He checked the top and bottom of the track either side of us, the hedge, then quickly dropped his arm. 'The thing is,' he lowered his voice and took a step closer, 'you were right. It wasn't an accident. But it wasn't because Billy was *White* or I was either.' He peered down at his wrist and scraped his thumbnail over the flat, pale scar, scrutinising it. 'I was *Black 4* when it happened. Nothing to be ashamed of.'

'*Black 4*. When was that then?' Not that it mattered.

'Two years ago.' His green eyes, with their engrossed expression, moved from the scar and rolled across the sky. 'It doesn't mean I have decades though. My rate could be faster. I could be well into grey now. Who knows.'

'I didn't ask to compare you to me,' I assured, guessing *I* was the same shade two years ago and probably a bit lighter than he would be now since I was a year younger. 'I asked to find out *when* you did it. So now, *why* did you do it?'

'Two reasons. One, so no one has to wait for me to die...'

'—Wait for you to die? You'll probably live into your 80's.'

'I mean *wait* for it to turn lighter. Wait for white. *Death.*' He flinched a shoulder as though it were obvious. 'Without a dot, people don't know what my shade is. They don't know how long to wait for. So they don't. And who would have thought that because they don't, they can't help but treat me like I have all the time in the world.' He seemed to delight in this deception, forgetting that he was better off getting through his youth with a dark mole.

'But it's *white*...'

'It's not actually white, Ivy—*it's* a scar.'

He stared at me like he was waiting for something—waiting for me to finally understand. But all I could think was my first impression of Teddy in the distance, on the crag, arms out, readying to dive into complete and utter brokenness. As far as I was concerned at the time, it *was* white. How might the next person catching only a glimpse see a mere scar—a scar that would be with him for the rest of his life?

'When they realise it's only a scar,' he explained, 'they don't hold anything against you. In fact, they almost feel bad you don't know where you are on the scale.'

Just like *I* had felt bad for him, I realised. What else was I supposed to feel about the glaring spot that ironically removed all indication of the real white to come.

'But they probably only feel bad because they genuinely believed it was an accident,' I pointed out. 'They'd probably feel differently if they knew you removed it on purpose.'

Teddy frowned and indignantly straightened his posture.

'Would they?' he challenged coolly, increasing his distance from me. 'Do *you*?'

'Well of course I don't—and I made that clear from the start, didn't I?' I reminded. 'Your colour doesn't matter at all.'

'Yes, but what if you found out I wasn't *Black 4* two years ago? What if I told you I was *Grey 9*?'

'It wouldn't matter,' I said flatly, ignoring the fact that

he not only lied to me about how his dot disappeared in the first place, but that it was quite possible he was further along his progression than he was willing to reveal—possibly even knew. 'I'd be *sad* probably if I found out you didn't have long, but not *angry*. I'd still want to be around you no matter.' I waited a beat, grappling with the point I had been trying to make about accidental removal versus intentional. 'But *sad* for one person just might be *angry* for another,' I tried articulating the difference between me, and those like Char's mum. 'There are some out there who will assume you got rid of your mole on purpose—their first thought will be that you did it to deceive them. To hide how far you are.'

Teddy looked at me long and hard for a moment, glanced back down the track, then squared with me.

'Do you feel deceived Ivy?'

By a young Transient's means of survival…?

'No.'

Not after Jack.

'What do you feel then?'

My throat quickened shut.

'What do you feel when you see my scar—where a mortality mole should be?' he pressed.

I swallowed hard.

'Well… I feel… relieved. Yes. *Relief* is what I feel seeing your mark there,' I said firmly, meaning it.

A wry, weary smile came over Teddy just then.

'Ivy the only reason anyone should feel relief… is because they prefer ignorance to fear.'

I wasn't sure whether to be offended or not.

'Don't worry,' he insisted, smiling sincerely now, 'everyone does. Even me. Why do you think I did it in the first place? For that very reason. I didn't want to be afraid of it getting lighter... I didn't want to see family worry, like they had already with Billy. I felt complete relief when I did it, and when everyone realised there was nothing that could be done, they did too.'

If this had been the benefit alone for Teddy to remove his dot, I could see now that it had been worth it—worth the ambiguity of a white scar until he got past those crucial years and into his late 20's. And of course, if he kept his wrist covered when he was outside his community of hard-working Transients, there was no need to worry about being mistaken for white.

It occurred to me just then that Teddy said there were two reasons he removed his dot.

'And the other reason you got rid of it?'

'Because I'm a Transient,' he said obviously. 'Eliminating one major thing people use to target and judge me cuts my battles by half. So now, I may have a white scar that makes someone do a double-take, but for the most part, I can hide it,' he admitted plainly, confirming what I had already imagined was the case. 'But what I can't hide beneath a sleeve is the fact that I move from one farm to another all year round... that I don't go to the local school... I don't fit in with...' he looked towards Trebullan, the sea '... this community— or any just like it. So there's no covering up the fact that I'm likely to be on the outskirts of society for my entire life... and I don't exactly have the option of tinting myself the least offensive colour at the local parlour,' he smirked, looking himself up and down, presenting his tanned skin in its entirety, 'now do I?'

'No. I guess not.'

It occurred to me just then that I had completely underestimated what the possibility of white meant for

Transients. Young Transients.

'We just don't have much of a choice Ivy.'

Seeing his kindly, flat smile there, I misunderstood him for a second and thought he meant he and I—*all of us* who were young didn't have much of a choice—that we all shared the WhitePlight the same—that he and I shared this struggle with mortality moles and social acceptance, *together*.

But of course he couldn't possibly have meant that, and I felt ashamed for even thinking his troubles were no different from mine.

Chapter Twenty-Three

Sorry

'I had no idea this is what you felt when your Gran died.' Char squinted up at me.

I wouldn't have been able to explain this feeling to her. How could I?

'Yeah well I'm sorry you have to go through it too now Char.'

But for some reason, I was a little glad I hadn't been the only one to feel such loss, or that ache at your insides like a worm was slowly hollowing you out. For once, it seemed Charlotte and I felt the same about something that really mattered.

'Death is horrible,' I said flatly, finding myself sinking slightly down the side of the dune. 'Which is why I couldn't quite make sense of the whole Good-bye Celebration thing.' I tried back-crawling up it a bit.

Char dug her heels into the sliding top layer of sand too and shifted her backside a few feet to the flatter top of the dune next to me.

'Yeah well I get that now,' she said blandly, pulling a straw of grass which she then began pinching off at the tip with her fingernails. 'The thing is, I can see what you mean about Good-bye Celebrations being a bit pointless when everyone's been expecting white—like for grandparents and whatever,' her head shook slightly, disagreeing with something, someone, 'but I'd still liked to have gone to Jack's.'

'Of course you would have. And you should have.'

As I sat and watched Char decimate the length of grass into tiny fragments only to grab another and begin doing the same, I realised I might have felt differently about Gran's Good-bye Celebration had the opportunity been taken away from me. For some of the more distant relatives, the ones who didn't feed and bathe Gran and tuck her into bed at the end of each day, it would have been their last chance of seeing her there in the garden... watching peacefully as the children played their games.

'I'm sorry you didn't get to go Char.'

'It's okay. Jack and I,' she looked at me and smirked, 'we're getting our own back.'

'I saw it was over 700 on my way back here,' I noted, getting out my phone.

'757.'

'Seriously?' I checked again. She was right. 757, 639 views. Just under 700,000 likes. No dislikes. No one dared. Not in the wake of this momentum. Not with this topic. 'Has your mum said anything else to you, texted you or anything?'

'Nope.'

We sat there in silence for a bit, watching the sea

birds circle around the rock in the distance off shore and I couldn't help think what a shame it had been that Char and her mother were at odds all because of the colour of someone's dot. A dot Sara paid close attention to every day in her line of work so that those in their week of white didn't face it alone. I couldn't imagine her doing her job well now. The White Wards required compassion. They demanded empathy. What would she do if someone like Jack ended up in one of her clinics?

'Do young people end up on the White Wards?' I broke our silence, wondering. 'You know, like the homeless... orphans or whatever.'

'No,' Char said regretfully. 'Young and on the streets... they just get brought to the back entrance for disposal. Their homeless friends or whatever can't pay the fees, so they just leave them. And *orphans*?' she scoffed. 'What, is this like... *Victorian* times or something?'

'Well *I* don't know...'

'*Foster* children...' Char enunciated with a tired smirk 'are looked after by the government. They get everything they need in the end.'

'Sor-ry...'

Playfully nudging me sideways with her shoulder, Char showed only a fraction of her old self and immediately reverted back to a leaden expression that showed the inevitable preoccupation of her thoughts.

'That's probably why she hates them,' she said gloomily all of a sudden. 'She probably hates the young and white because the only experience she actually has of them is the hassle they leave her under a dirty sheet or *IKEA* box on the back step.'

'They're just *left*? And she *told* you about them?'

'She tells me *everything* Ivy,' Char said pointedly, wiping her hands free of grass debris. 'How their mates don't care enough to even leave a name... how their mother clearly didn't want them—*for a reason*... how she chooses the cheapest option not to save the wards money, but because that's what young and white *deserve*....'

'Geez Char... she says that?'

She had gone to that place again that I had seen her go on the bench.

'That's not even the half of it....'

Again we were quiet.

'I wish we didn't have dots,' I said after a while, thinking of Teddy and his scar. 'I wish we didn't know when we'd die... and that people didn't think about death all the time.' Of course, it occurred to me that Billy's family benefitted when they found his dot had turned. But that was the exception. 'I wish that we had some other way of knowing we were about to go, that it was private somehow... that when it was about to happen, no matter how old you were, people cared. People thought it was all *a shame*. Because we all have to go through it—all of us.'

Charlotte didn't comment.

'You know that bloke I was with at the falls.' She looked up at me then. 'He doesn't have a dot. Sliced off in a farming accident.'

'Lucky him,' she remarked with no enthusiasm.

'When he was about to dive, the white we saw was his scar.'

Charlotte bit her lip and directed her attention to the dark under layers of dampened sand exposed around her imprint in the dune.

'Listen Ivy. About that picture….'

'I know you didn't mean it.'

'I didn't really think about what that boy's family—'

'—Seriously Char, you don't need to say anything.'

'No I do.' She twisted her body around, sinking a foot below me and looked up against the sun again. 'I was angry about my mum… and Jack… and the last thing I wanted was for you to find someone else—someone I knew would reject me.'

'Reject you?'

Hesitating, she sighed.

'That bloke saw Jack and me a few times up at the farm,' she confessed. 'He saw us taking stuff.'

'You?' It never crossed my mind that Jack got Charlotte go with him on his trips up to the Transients' caravans.

I realised just then that Teddy made no mention of it. And what was more, he hadn't been unkind to me despite knowing Char and I were friends.

'I guess you could just give it back,' I suggested, knowing she would want nothing to do with those things now. Not after Billy in that photo.

'I will—I want to—I can't bear any of it in the house now. But I'll be honest, my gut reaction for a minute there was *tit for tat*.'

I frowned, not following.

'You know, *me* taking *his* stuff, *him* taking *mine*. I hated it when Melissa and Georgia said you were with him again and I knew he'd tell you everything Jack and I did….'

'Listen Char, he didn't tell me anything. The only thing he ever said about either of you was that he recognised Jack from the news, and that once Jack was looking for us told him our names.'

'He *knows* my name...?'

I suddenly wished I had left out that distressing bit of information.

'Did you tell him about the photo—does he know about *that* then?'

'No of course not—no one knows about the photo except you and whoever Melissa and Georgia have sent it to,' I lied. 'Did you send it to anyone else, you know, with the comment attached?'

'Thankfully no. And I deleted it earlier. Georgia and Melissa though... well who knows who they've shared it with. I told them that in memory of Jack—in memory of anyone young and white—Transient or not—have a little respect and delete it.'

'What did they say?'

'Well they *said* they did. But they say a lot of stuff Ivy, don't they?' Char closed her eyes and sighed. 'Again, I wish I never sent it to you....'

It's okay....'

'No it's not okay. It's precisely the type of thing my mother would have done.'

'Char, you're not your mother.'

'No. I'm not.' She set her jaw for a moment then softened slightly. 'I made a mistake sending you that picture. I was angry Ivy. And I'm really sorry I did it.'

Her eyes began to water there against the wind and sun.

'I forgive you Charlotte.'

I'd never said those words to her before. But then, she had never said sorry to me.

Chapter Twenty-Four

Heirlooms

While we were on the dune, Jack's parents texted Char and invited her to come over.

'What do you think they want?' she looked up from her phone, worried.

'Well they probably know about the page,' I guessed, 'they probably know you wanted to go to Jacks celebration, that's all. I can't imagine it's anything to worry about.'

'But what if they didn't like what I put up? What if they didn't like the fact that I put *his letter* up—what if they thought that was too private?' she considered frantically. 'I mean what if they're upset about his story going viral?'

'Seriously Char, stop. Have you forgotten that they used the school gym and an open invitation for Jack's Good-bye? Had they been the kind of parents who would have wanted their white teen to keep hiding his colour, they wouldn't have done any of that. They'd of done like those families commenting on Jack's page—

hidden it. Kept it quiet.'

Char seemed to accept this, looked thoughtfully back to the text and wrote back.

Half an hour later, I waved her off from the bottom of the Fenner's drive and then went on to Madame's, who asked if I had heard about the trending local boy Jack. When I explained it all, told her the Charlotte who set up the page had a mother who worked on the White Wards... prevented her own daughter from attending the Good-bye Celebration of not just a classmate, but a close friend... and that the page wasn't just about the WhitePlight for young people like Jack, but people like Charlotte too... Madame's hostility towards the Char I had moaned and confided about completely disappeared once she realised they were one and the same. And when I told her that Charlotte had actually apologised... meaningfully... for the first time ever...

'Such contact with death makes one realise the futility of many things,' she tutted, poised with disinfectant and a rag beside the chair. 'I think there is no need for Antony now,' she concluded. 'This Charlotte, she has deep regret, deep shame. We must forgive.'

I watched Madame move resolutely on to the next table and as she scrubbed, wiped and sprayed, I thought of the things Char had from the Transients, the stuff she and Jack took that she now wanted to return. This I mentioned to Madame.

'After everything with Jack, and her mum, I don't know where she'd even get the courage to go up and give everything back.' I blinked with eyes wide, trying to picture Charlotte laden with bags, walking along that dirt track to the caravans, ogled by children and farmhands. A walk of shame.... To then explain it all, confess it....

'Perhaps you can leave the items here,' Madame suggested. 'I have tea with the farmer's wife. I can explain things.'

The thought of Char being spared the humiliation of returning everything herself made me want to take Madame's offer on her behalf then and there. But before I leaped at the reprieve, it crossed my mind that maybe Char *wanted* to experience the shame, wanted to face it and put it right. With the way she had properly mended things with me, was facing Jack's death and her mother, albeit on a global scale... I really had no idea what was going on in my best friend's head.

'I don't know how she's going to sort it out to be honest. That's really kind of you to offer though, but Char might just want to do it all herself. You know, so she doesn't have a guilty conscience about someone else doing it for her.' But then, what if she *wanted* to remain anonymous? 'I don't know... I mean, I'll mention it to her. See what she says.'

Madame pushed the chairs in around her last table then came to where I stood, beside the little milk and sugar table.

'I can assure you Ivy,' she narrowed in on me, making me uncomfortable slightly, 'if this Charlotte brings the things here that she has taken, she will not leave with a guilty conscience. And she can be confident all of it will be returned to its rightful owner.' She retreated, returned to the counter and shrugged dismissively. 'Of course, it is up to her.'

I hadn't realised how keen Charlotte was to get rid of everything because no sooner had I met her at the end of my road and told her what Madame said—*how* she said it, so pointedly and all—she left me in complete shock at the suggestion that we go down to the Plughole right then and there to drop a bag off.

'C'mon, before it closes Ivy,' she urged, pulling me in the direction of the seafront.

'But customers...' I spluttered, holding back, not wanting anyone to see her in broad daylight with stolen goods. 'We can take it later. After dark.'

'But I've got it *now*,' she breathed, to which I looked her straight frame up and down, looked at the nearly transparent shopping bag with only a few items of her clothing in.

'Now? *Where?*'

She shushed me and looked over her shoulders up and down the street.

'I've just taken back some stuff from Jack's room,' she whispered. 'Stuff *he* had taken,' and stopping beside the curb, I glanced dubiously at the bag in her hand once more. There was nothing there but an item or two of clothing. I then eyed the rest of her more carefully. Finding she had no apparent lumps or bumps, or bulging pockets, I asked again,

'*Where?*'

Quickly, she dashed ahead and up the steps, waving me to hurry and unlock the front door. With Mum still snoring, Charlotte strode over to the dining table, and to my astonishment, pulled out a long, thin, blue velvet necklace box from the back of her jeans. She opened it and showed me its pearl contents. Setting it on the table, she then took a men's wrist watch from her pocket, an antique mother of pearl hairbrush from the inside of her boot, a fabric pull-string bag full of earrings out of her other pocket, and a child's diary from under her shirt.

'*Charlotte...*' I hissed, looking at the pile of what clearly was someone's treasure. 'Someone's *diary...?*'

'I know…. But wait a minute—this was *Jack's*.' Jack's loot she made clear. 'I couldn't just leave it now could I? Half of it I didn't even know he took until I saw it in there. And they said they *knew* it wasn't his… they *wanted* me to go in there and take what didn't belong to him.' She stared up at the ceiling and felt her pockets and along her belt for anything more. 'I know it sounds crazy to take it all, but what was I supposed to do? They said they were going to *give away* some of his stuff—basically they would have given away what *wasn't* actually Jack's. And I had this horrible thought when they told me, that they'd have a boot sale and someone would find out this was all stolen… and then everything *horrible* that people wanted to believe about young and white… well it would mean they'd all have just another reason to hate *Jack*.' Char looked at the diary, poked it so the cover faced her the right way round. 'I couldn't leave it all up there, now could I?'

No, she couldn't.

'I seriously almost did though, because I thought, if I take all this back, give it back to the Transients… what if a Transient then was seen with it?' She picked up the men's watch. 'You know, what if Mr Fenner knew I took this away with me and then saw it on one of the men up there and thought *they* stole it from *me*?'

'That's unlikely Char.' I couln't imagine the Fenners, both Professors at the local college, coming into contact with any Transient. '*Teachers* and *Transients*?' I offered sarcastically.   'Besides, these items, they're… well… personal. The kind of stuff you keep in a bedside table or something. Not laying about, and certainly not wearing everyday.' I hated the thought of Jack rummaging around in what could have been Teddy's own home to find this lot, and I was really beginning to hate the look of it scattered over the dining table.

'Yeah well, I had a peek at the diary when I was deciding what to take, like *they* no doubt did,' Char confessed, 'and it's obvious it belongs to a Transient. I think they *wanted* me to go up and get not just *my* things, but anyone else's I knew should go back where it belonged.'

I was confused, and slightly disappointed at the thought of the Fenners' inviting Char around soley to collect their son's spoils from the farm.

'So they didn't talk to you about Jack, or have you over for a cup of tea or whatever then?'

'No we had a drink and a chat. In fact, they were really lovely about the whole Good-bye Celebration thing, about me not being able to go. And I have their full support with the page. But they said there were things in his room still they knew belonged to me. And they thought it would be a nice gesture to let me be in his room since I wasn't able to get to the gym. On my own for a bit. You know, to say good-bye I guess, seeing as they're clearing it all out tomorrow. I thought it was kind actually.' She sighed then half-smiled, prompting me to do the same, for it was no different to Gran. White, and then the big clearout. 'They said it was the best they could do in his absence and all, and after we cried, well, they gave me a bag and let me go in and take what was mine. *And anything else that might need to go back to its owner* they said, when they came in to see how I was getting on. Thankfully, I had already loaded up by then. They had it all setting out in the open.' She rolled her eyes at the items on the table and said frankly, 'They *knew*.'

'Well then they're probably glad it's out of the house then.'

'Probably.'

'Then you don't really need to worry about them seeing any of this on a Transient, not if they already know one item belongs to them,' I figured, nodding to the diary.

'No, I guess I don't.'

'And you don't want to take any of this up to Churley's yourself?'

'Ivy, if *I* had taken this, then I would,' she insisted. 'But *Jack* took it. And I'm not about to go up there and say that it was *me* or *by the way, this is what* I *took, and this is what my friend* Jack *took. Sorry he couldn't be here to return it himself but....'*

'Okay—I get it.'

'Listen,' she glanced over to the ceiling where Mum could still be heard snoring, 'I took stuff that could *easily* be replaced. Now I'm not saying that to make it sound less wrong, but I've never taken anything that was obviously personal. And I certainly would never take someone's *diary.'* She picked up the velvet necklace box and looked inside again. 'The last thing I wanted to take was an heirloom.' She snapped it shut. 'So if I can drop *this stuff* off to the shop as soon as possible—knowing the person who wants it back will get it sooner—because my plan otherwise was just to do an anonymous drop-off sometime—*then great*. But the things *I've* taken, I'll go and return them myself. Properly. Face whoever I need to.' Her shoulders dropped and she rolled her eyes. 'Of course, it's all stashed in *my room....'*

She clearly hated the thought of returning home.

'Do you want me to come with you, to the shop and everything?'

She bit her lip, looking uncertain.

'Ivy, I know this is the last thing you want to do, but if you would, I'd be really grateful.'

I appreciated that she took some consideration as to how I might feel aiding and abetting someone with stolen goods. The Char from yesterday certainly would not have.

167

'Of course.' As far as I was concerned, the sooner she sent it all back, the better. 'I've got Madame's number,' I remembered, reminding her it had been Gran's phone when she frowned. 'I'll see if we can drop it all off later. After Mum goes to work?'

Char nodded and I started texting.

'She's happy for us to come by the shop tonight after hours,' I relayed a moment later.

'I'll go and get the other stuff then' Char moaned, 'and I should probably make an appearance for dinner.' Her tall frame shrunk a few inches and she threw her head back clearly dreading another encounter with her mother. 'Hopefully I can be back here sometime around 8. Can I leave all this with you in case she has something else up her sleeve when I get in?' She nodded to the trove on the table.

'Yeah, sure. I mean, I can take it all to the Plughole myself if you'd rather, or if you don't end up getting away.'

'No I'd like to do it. I sort of feel like I'm the only one who can make apologies for Jack,' she explained. 'I just don't want to have to bring it back with me in case I get a load of questions.'

'Okay.'

'Shall we say 8:30 then?'

I quickly confirmed 8:45pm with Madame.

'She'll be expecting us at the back door.'

Char picked up the plastic bag she got from the Fenners with what looked like a cardigan and scarf and, no doubt focused on the battle zone waiting at home, headed out the door without a word.

I texted Madame that if Char got tied up, we'd reschedule, then I put everything on the kitchen table in a compost bin bag and stuffed it into my backpack in the hall.

Chapter Twenty-Five

Ignorance

The top was a bit burnt, the edges of the pepperoni mostly, but Mum didn't complain.

'So Charlotte actually apologised.' Impressed, she took an awkward bite of her pizza and let the crust crack and fall all over her plate, oblivious-like. 'Now tell me again, you sent her a message about Jack and she decided to meet up with you?'

I went through everything again, but in greater detail, telling her how I went to the bench and texted Char that I was sorry to hear Jack had died—the same bench he had pranked us and where he probably decided he did have to tell everyone what his true colour was. But of course, Char was on her way to the same place, I explained.

'She wanted to be on her own there for a bit, so came back this way.' I left the bit out about meeting Teddy on the track beside the farm and instead told her how I met up with Char later on the dunes and that it was then that she properly apologised to me for the comment she sent with the picture.

'Did you tell her Camille dragged you off to go and tell the police?'

'No. She didn't need to know. Becasue as far as I'm concerned, it's all done and dealt with.' I was almost certain that had Char any concerns as to what I'd tell the police, it would have more to do with the stash in my bag on the floor by the door than a comment alongside a photo she had already apologised for. And I left out too that it was Char's shame in seeing me with Teddy—becasue of that stash—that fuelled the angry text she sent in the first place. 'I think she's sorting things out now,' I went on. 'She got Melissa and Georgia to delete the picture of Teddy with his little brother—at least, she's hoping they did… and when I saw Madame later, after she realised Charlotte was the same person who set up Jack's page, she seemed to think Char was really sorry about the whole thing and saw there was no point in taking things further.'

'Good,' Mum said firmly, evidently relieved. 'Camille is an emotionally driven woman, but I'm glad to see she has a sensible degree of restraint. There would be no benefit in telling Charlotte that picture was taken perhaps more seriously than was probably necessary.' Mum caught my eye, indicting Madame Laurent for leading me off to Antony Harley in his police shed only to be told nothing could be done.

'I'm just glad it's gone,' I sighed, and eager to forget that horrible image, I hastily moved on and told her about Char's visit to the Fenners'. Minus the stolen goods.

'Oh Ivy…' Mum gushed 'you know what…' she put her petrified slice of pizza down '…those two… they have been *examples* to this community,' she declared. '*Real* examples. They've impressed me with how they handled everything with Jack… and now to recognise Charlotte had a role in his life… and to support what she's done after his death….' She shook her head, picked up her spoon and started scooping baked beans like she couldn't believe she was doing so. 'Seriously…. If only Sara could show the same compassion to her daughter that pretty much *strangers* have…. I mean, Charlotte's not even *white*,' Mum remarked. 'You know her views have gone well over 800,000' she digressed.

'I know,' I marvelled, pulling my phone out and confirming it. '866,431.'

'Has her mum said anything about the memorial page?'

'I think she resents Charlotte for having a voice she can't just shut away in a bedroom,' I suspected. 'You know her colleagues at the Wards have been putting comments up.'

'Yes, I saw. Condemning her actions, when she should *be a veteran of compassion*.' Mum gave me a heeding look. 'I think it's given the staff room over there a little shake up, don't you think?'

'*Something*. But seriously Mum, you wouldn't believe the horrible stuff she says about young and white to Char. I really have no idea why she's working there.'

'Because most of her patients are old, Ivy. Old and have had a full life. For the most part, they face white gracefully, with dignity, and they're not much work. People who think they shouldn't be there—those who feel short-changed in life—the ones who feel society shaming them for what is clearly out of their hands— well they don't exactly face white quietly, do they?'

Mum flashed a knowing look, causing me believe she knew more about what went on in those White Wards just outside our tiny little village than was wise to tell me.

'I think Sara's afraid really,' I decided. 'Afraid a bunch of *yoofs* are going to track her down and break her—put her in hospital til she turns white.'

'Youths, huh?' Mum rolled her eyes at the ridiculousness of it. 'Unfounded fear Ivy,' she took a gulp from her mug and threw her eyebrows up to the ceiling. 'Ignorance.'

Finishing my dinner, I thought of Sara's fear, the things Char told me about her hatred of anyone our age, turning. I pictured her breaking and ending up in hospital, ironically relying on under-30's to assist with her mending, under-30's who were possibly lighter than her.... And I thought too about Teddy's scar, Teddy having been in hospital, because, presumably, when he sliced off his mole, he would have ended up in A&E.

'I saw someone without their mortality mole today,' I changed the subject, trying not to sound too light and airy. 'A builder. Down by the seafront,' I lied.

Mum didn't seem phased by the shift in conversation as she finished off her beans.

'If it was an accident, wouldn't he have gone to see you?' I asked casually. 'On account of the blood and all.'

'One of us,' Mum reckoned. 'But he could have sorted it with a plaster I imagine. *Pressure and plaster,*' she said thoughtlessly like a little rhyme. Like it happens all the time.

My blasé expression furrowed with concern.

'Do... *lots* of people lose their dots then,' I asked carefully.

'Not really, no. Pressure and plaster is for anything

small. You know, so you don't have to come in in the first place,' she explained, 'you know—it's the advice we give over the phone.'

'So you don't get a lot of mole-related injuries?'

'No, Love,' she answered plainly. 'The hospital tends to get things that end up being life-changing. Broken bones… limbs removed, regrown… nerve regeneration, transplants… that sort of thing. We help people cope with whatever level of brokenness they have. Reduce it, because—'

'—*They'll have to live with it til they're white*,' I finished the heeding sentence I had heard and read a million times in school, out and about, and heard plenty of at home.

'Indeed.' She gave me a consoling smile.

'But what about people *so* broken?' I tried getting my head round. 'I mean, have there been people so broken that like, say they had their head chopped off or crushed or something.'

'All fixable,' she determined.

'And they don't *die*—like a crushed bug or something— they don't turn white then and there?'

'Love, they're not *insects,* and they're not *animals*,' she insisted. 'They're broken. That's all. I mean, some will be more broken than others, but just because they might never be the same doesn't mean they're as good as white. If anything, spending time in hospital reminds people that it's a waste of time—maybe even shades— ending up there, so they're a bit more careful once they get out.'

'It's crazy…' I scoffed. 'How is it that we can put creatures out of their misery, yet we can't do that for ourselves?'

'But we *do* put people out of their misery Ivy,' she however pointed out. 'The healing process that takes place in hospital—that is the misery being taken away.'

'Yeah, but not if the thing that put you there in the first place is still waiting for you when you hobble out,' I argued. 'I mean, isn't it like you said? Some injuries could change you for life. And what if you walk out of there only to face the very thing that got the ambulance coming for you in the first place? Wouldn't that then be the source of your misery—wouldn't *that* be the very thing the hospital can do absolutely nothing about?' I was desperate for her to see that brokenness didn't always happen at the snap of a bone, or the poor function of an organ. 'And what about the person who could hide how miserably broken they were…?'

Like Jack.

Teddy.

'I see your point,' Mum sighed patiently. 'Listen,' she relented, 'I can't change the fact that we die when we're white and that until then, we have to get on with our suffering. I can't change the fact that we can put creatures out of their misery, ending their lives in an arbitrary instant, while the rest of us have no quick and compassionate way out. I don't know why we're different from them, but we are.' The corners of her mouth dragged up a smile. 'Perhaps *we're* the lucky ones Ivy, knowing when we'll die. Surely it's better to know than live in complete ignorance.'

The word caught me just then.

Ignorance.

'No, I don't want to be ignorant,' I asserted, distracted vaguely by the word still.

Seeing that we were both finished, Mum stacked

our plates and cutlery and took it all to the sink.

'Mum...?'

'Hmm?'

'Do people try and get rid of their dots?' I no longer felt such a question had to surface from a lie; a scarred builder I might have spotted by the seafront.

'Yes Ivy,' she told me, turning around. 'Yes they do.' She shrugged. 'Of course they do. People in desperate situations do desperate things, don't they?'

'Desperate situations? Like what?'

She surveyed the room for a second, apparently thinking of the least shocking answer. 'Like being white in your 30's... trying to remove white from your child....' My eyes widened, aghast. 'Yep. People try.'

'Do they do it to teens—do parents do it to their own...'

'—No, not teens.'

'Do teens do it to themselves then?' I couldn't help ask the question that had been burning in my mind nearly a week now. 'Do they come in, you know... people Jack's age,' Teddy's 'having tried to get rid of it?'

'Do you know,' she said thoughtfully, 'no one comes in between the ages of 13 and 30. It's either younger or older. Parent-inflicted for the younger, and self-inflicted for the older.' She stared at me for a second, curious. 'Young people don't like to stand out for the wrong reasons, Ivy. I hadn't really thought about it before, but I imagine that 13-30 group is what keeps the tinting parlours in business, don't you?'

Wanting my question to appear as a whim, I brought the mugs over and said dismissively,

'I guess.' Then more cheerfully, 'Oh, I meant to mention, Char's going to come over a bit later, if that's alright. Not to stay the night. Just to hang out.'

'That's fine Love.' Mum sounded glad to be talking about something else. 'I don't blame her for wanting to spend as little time as possible in that bedroom of hers.'

After Mum left for work, I thought more about that word.

Ignorance.

Teddy had pointed out on the track that the only reason I wasn't rejecting him with his scar... the only reason I confessed to being relieved by it... was because I had been ignorant of his true colour. *That* was the ignorant I was afraid to be—the ignorant that might feel differently towards him had I known his real shade.

Yet because of this, because of the fear white created in me, a part of me *wanted* to be completely ignorant. So ignorant that death dots and colour would mean nothing to me anymore. Not just my own... but everyone else's around me.

Part of me wanted to be like Teddy, whose lack of a mortality mole meant he no longer compared himself to others, judged others... and found that people could no longer judge him on account of what he didn't have.

While I waited for Char to arrive, I tried imagining myself ignorant of *Black... Grey... White...*. I tried thinking of what I'd regret, being so ignorant. What Teddy surely regrets, after Billy.

Chapter Twenty-Six

Plughole

I opened the door and found Charlotte standing there with a thunderstruck look on her face.

'What *happened*?' I asked, daunted, closing the door as she headed straight for the kitchen with her bags of loot.

'We're moving,' she said flatly when I came in from the hall.

'*Moving*? Who's moving?'

'*We are.* My mother and me.'

My middle felt as though it had become a void. An empty, immeasurable vacuum.

'Are you serious?'

'The house is already on the market apparently,' Char informed with annoyance. 'It seems that while my mother was off today with stress, she decided it was best we move to Exeter.'

'Exeter? Why Exeter?'

'Because it's a city.' She put the bags on the table. 'Because *you can be anonymous in a city,*' she mocked, obviously quoting her mother.

'But that's rubbish...' I argued '...she'll need to get another job... people will *know* who she is—people will know who *you* are,' it occurred to me. 'They'll be looking for you both if *you* suddenly disappear—there's no way she can hide then.

'Well she's applied to change her name. And she's going to delete my account—any online presence I have as soon as she gets the password off me.'

There was no way Sara could sell up and ditch town with a daughter in tow who had an online following well up to a million now.

'And when will you give her the password?' I expected her to say never.

'When the broadband stops in 48 hours and the cancellation of my phone account goes through.'

I was the one looking thunderstruck now.

'...But she can't...she just can't....'

'She can Ivy, and she will.'

'But what about *school*... your friends... what about Jack's page....'

'She says she's sorting school. And you're my only real friend Ivy. I'll keep in touch, I promise. And as for my online account, Jack's parents were really understanding. Maybe they'll open a new page I can manage from school or something, or a library once we're settled.'

'*How* can you be accepting this?' I asked incredulously, certain there was no way Sara would allow her daughter to even get near The Fenners, much less communicate with them in months to come regarding Jack. In fact, I was

almost certain Jack's parents were the type
even dare put Char in such an awkward positi
mother.

'Well it's all my fault, isn't it?' she said dismal
wasn't sure if she believed her own words or not. 'Sh
can't go back to work because I told everyone how she
banned me from going to Jack's Good-bye Celebration.
And after everything I put up just *now*...' she admitted,
flinching a shoulder, giving me the impression all her
followers would soon find out she was moving, 'well she's
getting death threats because I aired our dirty laundry for
the world to see.' She gave a pathetic smile.

There was no doubt, she did believe it was all her fault.

'But Char, the only reason you didn't go to Jack's
do was because *she's* got a thing against young and
white. That's not *your* fault.'

'I didn't have to tell the world though, did I?' She
peeked blankly into the top of a few bags. 'Listen Ivy,
one thing at a time. Can we just sort this stuff out?' she
urged, nodding to the goods. 'I can't have any of it in
the house now. And don't we need to be down there'
she checked the clock on the wall 'in like five minutes?'

My head rattled for a second and I swiftly went
and took what Char handed me.

As we walked down to the Plughole, I couldn't
get out of my mind that all this running, this fleeing...
was because of a stupid dot on the wrist. A dot I could
hardly make out was white or black in the dim, cobbled
alleyways down to the backdoor of Madame Laurent's.

I watched Charlotte stiffen and blow out a nervous
puff of air after I knocked.

'You okay?'

'Fine. Let's just get this done with.'

a t h   D o t

l the door from the other side
ushed voice. She led us to the
st the till and offered us a drink,
I politely declined.

need to beat about the bush as
lling out a chair and joining us.
u would like to return to their
rected to Char.

hree of the bags beside her feet
towards Madame with her chin to her chest, ashamed.
'I need to take this one up to Churley's myself,' she
however indicated the single bag the other side of her.

'Take it up yourself?' Madame confirmed, looking
slightly confused.

Char's eyes darted from side-to-side across the
table and I could tell she was trying to find the right
words, but with incredible difficulty.

'Those are the things *Jack* has taken,' I emphasised,
explaining on Char's behalf.

Here, Madame's brow lifted high, softening her
quizzical expression. 'I see. And presumably what
you have there is what *you* have taken.' She hesitated
tactfully. 'What you feel the need to return.'

'Yes.'

The three of us were suddenly startled by a heavy
knock at the back door.

'Are you expecting anyone?' I eyed Madame
distrustfully, worrying for a second that she decided to
invite Antony, the constable.

'Possibly...' she divulged to my disappointment,
then disappeared to the back.

I couldn't help throw a panicked look at Char. 'I
thought it was only the three of us,' I maintained quietly

180

to her, hearing a male voice enter the building.

Madame came in from the darkened rear of the shop and my heart leapt and fell flat at the sight of Teddy behind her—Teddy I had such fondness for... but Teddy whose brother's death had been mocked by my friend opposite me. It crossed my mind that he might have been unaware of the photo Char sent me, however, he most certainly would have recognised the girl in the room as having taken items from his relatives that ought to have been returned.

For the second time this evening, my gut hollowed out.

'Ivy... Charlotte,' Madame announced, 'I would like to introduce to you my grandson, Theodore.'

All of a sudden, Char burst into tears and cried out, 'I'm so sorry....' She buried her face in her arms on the table and sobbed the words over and over, '...I'm so sorry... I'm so sorry... I didn't mean to take any of it....'

Overwhelmed, and utterly confused by Madame's connection to Teddy, I spontaneously put an arm around Char's juddering shoulders, trying to sooth her, and watched as Teddy rushed over and knelt at her side. Then as he too put a hand on her back and told her that it was okay, that he knew this was a difficult thing to have to do, but that he wasn't angry with her... that she was doing the right thing, I thought of the same tenderness he had shown to his little brother at the falls. How devoted he was on the way up to the farm. The same kindness was no different to how he was with Char at that moment, and I found that I too was beginning to cry.

After a while, we all wiped our eyes and sat around the table, sheepishly looking at one another.

'So Teddy is your grandson?' I spoke first, seeing Madame's eagerness to drag me over to Antony's in a completely different light now. Because Teddy and Billy hadn't just been vulnerable Transients. They were family.

'Teddy's grandfather and I were together only a short while,' Madame revealed. 'Just before I married.' There was an awkward silence in the room, for everyone knew she didn't marry a Transient, and that she never had other children. 'Of course, I had to give him up…' she confessed, '…but the only ones who would have him… were Transients.' She looked at Teddy, apparently grateful for this, to which he then explained,

'They were forced to try and put Dad into foster care. Then adoption. All possibilities had to be ruled out before they'd consider a nomadic community.'

'But it was no use,' Madame went on with a tone of triumph. 'No one wanted a baby with a father *who wandered*.'

Teddy shrugged though, clearly glad this had been the case as Char and I looked at them both in amazement.

'We all have something to be ashamed of,' Madame said simply, pointedly, looking round the table. 'I wish I never gave up my son. And I wish I hadn't tried to cover up my shame in doing so by marrying a man I didn't love. A man who reminded me daily of who I would have been stuck with had it not been for his pity on me.' She gave Teddy a heavy, knowing look, to which he pursed a regretful smile. 'It was a person I wished every day I could have been stuck with.'

'Grandpa died when I was little,' Teddy said. 'But I still have Gran here,' he added gratefully.

'Some mistakes can still be mended,' she declared,

clearly delighting in the fact that her grandson was sitting beside her, acknowledging her relationship to him, something I got the impression was lacking between Teddy's father and Madame when he came into her shop during the downpour.

'So the man who came in here the other day…'

'My son,' she confirmed.

'Are you two not close then?' I asked carefully. 'Or was it just a front, for the locals?'

Madame hesitated before answering. 'We are *mending*, shall we say.' Putting her hands on the table, she folded them in front of her and turned to Char. 'It is never too late to try and mend things, is it not?'

Death Dot

Chapter Twenty-Seven

People

Teddy carried the bags. He told Charlotte, after a glance at the items, that he could see everything she brought belonged either to his family, cousins, aunts or uncles, and said she didn't need to go up to give any of it back. He would return it all himself, on her behalf. And Jack's.

A short while later, the three of us walked through the narrow, salty streets up to Anchor Road.

'This one's yours?' Teddy lifted his chin to Char's house on our approach.

'That's it,' Char declared blandly to the narrow two-story semi, armoured with sheets of slate.

I gasped all of a sudden as we slowed to the front gate, for I had just noticed the silhouette of boxes stacked in the hallway behind the frosted glass front door. The chink of kitchen light at the end of the hall made them appear as though the beginnings of a wall. A fortress, keeping Sara safe in her wi-fi-free dungeon.

'She's serious,' I uttered in disbelief, referring to the move Char had just told Teddy about on account of her online activity.

'And you wonder how I can accept it?' Char remarked, shaking her head hopelessly at the blocks of cardboard beyond the short front path.

'Charlotte,' Teddy said apprehensively, stopping her just before she went through the gate. 'Your natural instinct over what is right…' he hesitated, shifting up the bags in his hands '…and what is wrong….' He didn't finish. It was like he couldn't find the right words, or was afraid to say them. 'Your online activity has helped a lot of people, is what I'm trying to say,' he resolved. 'And there should be a way of doing it—of helping others, and remembering Jack's plight—without blaming your mother.'

Char recoiled and rolled her eyes, indignant.

'What I mean to say,' he hastened, 'is that she isn't to blame. Of course, she is responsible for her *own* actions,' he was quick to admit '—she injured you when she prevented you from seeing Jack… but I think what I'm trying to say is that she *alone* cannot be blamed for her attitude against young and white.' Seeing that Char wasn't buying any of it, Teddy's lips thinned, frustrated. 'I'm not saying she isn't without blame, by any means,' he tried again in earnest. 'But your followers want to blame *someone* for their experiences. And the only target you have given them is the person from yours.' Char's set features slackened slightly. 'Your mum can't possibly be the one responsible for all that now, can she?'

Char let out an exasperated sigh.

'I never said she was the one *responsible*,' she retorted. 'I said it was *minds like hers*….'

'Yes but those who feel they no longer have someone to blame—that the person who injured them can't pay... for whatever reason... then they will direct it...' he glanced in dismay at the glowing glass beyond '...they'll direct it to the same person you are. And from what you just said were your last posts... you've given them permission.'

We all stood there for a moment, silently looking at one another. The thought of Sara somehow taking on not just her daughter's sense of injustice over the WhitePlight, but every person who had a bad experience... around the globe potentially... well it seemed ludicrous. Counterproductive.

'What do you suppose I do then?' Char asked honestly, clearly willing to consider Teddy's advice not just on account of his generosity to her back at the Plughole, but because he was making some sense, and by the look of what was already stacked against Char in that doorway, the situation wasn't exactly getting any better. 'It's not like I can change the mind of *every* person who has an issue with young and white—in fact I don't even *know* who those people *are*,' she spat, whispering. 'But what I *do* know is that my mother despised my classmate— my *friend*—and she needs to know her way of thinking is *not* acceptable. So if she won't listen to me... then maybe she'll listen to friends and colleagues. *Strangers* even, if that's what it takes.'

Teddy's shoulders fell, disappointed that she hadn't understood him somehow.

'And where do you end up in all of that?' he said calmly. 'When she's fighting the masses, where is your voice then, the one that wanted her to listen when you couldn't go and see Jack?'

'Well this is all bigger than me now, isn't it?' Char dismissed sullenly.

'But it's not,' Teddy insisted. 'And this is what I'm *trying* to tell you. If you let your voice—your relationship with your mother—become lost in the rallying of followers… basically… you will already have lost your fight to gain her back. She won't see *you* anymore, her daughter. She will only see *them*, those strangers you mentioned. You'll end up sacrificing yourself to the many. And then who will *you* be—who will *she* be at the end of each day, in those quiet moments, when the followers are not there beside either of you, living in the same space only the two of you occupy?' He nodded to the illuminated door behind her, the rooms above. 'The battle with her then, it will become a stalemate. You won't have changed her at all, and isn't that what you were trying to do with all this in the first place?'

Charlotte folded her arms and stepped away from the gate.

'So what then?'

'Don't lose yourself in what you're leading online.'

'And how do I do that?'

'Engage with your mother using your own voice.'

'Yeah well she doesn't listen to me, remember?'

'Then listen to hers first.'

Char threw him a confused frown. 'I already know what she *thinks*,' she scoffed.

'And do you know why?'

'No….' Her indignation showed there was clearly no need to know why.

'Then that is where your battle is with her Charlotte.'

The sincerity, the humility behind Teddy's words disarmed her, and I had never seen my best friend so empty of retorts and remarks, especially on a subject concerning her mother.

'Understanding why your mother thinks what she does…' he went on, '…showing her empathy despite her views… that is where you maintain your voice and win her over,' he said firmly, kindly.

I couldn't tell what was going through Char's head just then, whether or not she thought there really was anything in Teddy's words, because at that point, she promptly thanked him for being willing to return the things she and Jack had taken, then went expressionless through her gate and up into the house. And Teddy said nothing more of it when he walked me home on the way back to the farm. However once we got to the end of Anchor Road and started up the steep hill to my street, I decided to tell him what Mum said about the people who ended up in A&E having tried to remove their dots.

'She said the ones under 13 are parent-inflicted, and the ones over 30 are self-inflicted. Basically she doesn't get anyone coming in in the middle.'

'Probably because they've figured a way of covering it by 13, and they're too desperate by 30,' Teddy remarked, spotting windows with lights on and curtains still open, silhouettes passing behind them. I got the impression as we made our way up the hill that he might not like being on his own in the village after dark.

'Well either way,' I carried on more quietly, 'she didn't seem to think it was a big deal, trying to remove it.'

He looked at me oddly just then.

'Your mum doesn't seem to think removing your mortality mole is a big deal?' he asked in disbelief, frowning.

'Only medically speaking—she's a nurse at the hospital,' I clarified, to which he threw back his head, understanding. 'But the thing is,' I went on, '...when I figured trying to remove a dot would require a trip down to A&E, she pretty much just said *pressure and plaster*. Pressure and plaster. Like it was no big deal. Like they didn't even need to go down there and see her.'

I waited, hoping Teddy would say something. Tell me what happened when he removed his own dot.

'I guess a plaster might make some feel better,' he granted, indifferent, divulging nothing. We turned right onto my road at the top of the hill and as I saw the terrace ahead, and the lamp over my front door now gathering moths, I decided to ask him directly,

'Did yours bleed when you took it off?'

Teddy stopped in the darkness between two dim street lights. He asked if I really wanted to know, to which I answered a solemn yes.

'It didn't bleed at all.'

'Did it hurt?'

'Not even a bit.' The plastic bags in each of his hands crinkled as he switched them over. 'Is that it?' he asked with a degree of finality that suggested there was nothing more to tell even if I did have another question.

'Yes, that was it,' I admitted, heading for the house.

Under the porch lamp, his bright eyes were like little beacons, attracting a curious insect or two. And with the gate between us, I suddenly didn't want him to go.

'Goodnight Teddy,' I couldn't think of anything else to say. 'Thank you.'

I regretted the words as soon as they came out.

'Goodnight Ivy.' Then as his lips pulled straight into a pleasant sort of expression, I thought for a second that actually he appeared sad. 'You're welcome.'

All of a sudden, I had that horrible feeling he was

about to disappear off into the darkness just as he had in the hedge.

'Will I see you again?' I asked impulsively the second he looked up the street.

'I'm sure you will.' He smiled like it was unlikely though.

I tried just then to think of a reason to see him again, but I had no need to go up to the farm, or its orchards. And it was doubtful that I'd see him working when I hadn't ever before. And our encounter on the track... well it had only happened because *he* was looking for *me*.

Perhaps Madame... I quickly thought, but it seemed unlikely when her own son wouldn't even accept a hot drink off her, in her own shop. It was no wonder then that she made her tea trips up to the farmer's wife, if that was her only glimpse of children and grandchildren. It occurred to me just then that Teddy's father might not have approved of his son coming to the Plughole and might even be up at the farm this very minute looking for him. Exhaling, my only other thought was the falls. Of course, Teddy had no need to go there now. Every reason not to, in fact.

'I hope so,' I said, disheartened, now wishing Transients each had their own mobile phones, though was resigned to the fact that they shared one out of necessity, like a land line.

'I hope so too Ivy.' Teddy looked down at his feet for an awkward second, then back to me. 'I should probably get back.'

He referred to the loot, lifting both hands a few inches.

'Yes, of course.'

Nodding politely he then disappeared up the road into the shadows between the streetlamps.

My dreams that night had me chasing him down a rabbit warren like *Alice's Adventures in Wonderland*, only I never saw him, yet somehow I knew he was there, around the next bend. And when I woke to Mum's heavy snoring, the same disorientation and certainty followed me, making me realise I hadn't heard her come in from her shift at all, and that I had slept in. I realised too as my phone vibrated against the mattress under the edge of my pillow that I had missed five of Char's messages:

When you wake, ring me. 9:09am

Are you awake??? 9:13am

I just tried ringing you and it goes to vm. Are you at home? 9:36am

Seriously Ivy, ring me as soon as you get this. 9:58am

Please look at this... 10:40am

She sent me a link to her page, which I clicked. It was a video headed *THIS ISN'T ABOUT WHITE—IT'S ABOUT PEOPLE.*

I immediately recognised Jack's parents walking up the path to Charlotte's house. The footage was being taken from an upstairs window. Then the camera hustled to the landing... the doorbell rang... and Charlotte's mother cautiously peeked through the frosted glass. She opened the door, stood boldly in the doorway but was clearly on her guard, recognising them. I couldn't make out what they were saying. Perhaps nothing was said. A subtext at the bottom of the video however popped up:

We just wanted to talk to you about Charlotte. And Jack.

At that moment, I watched as Sara did what I saw her daughter do last night. She wept and crumpled... and was caught by Mrs Fenner there in the doorway. She then cried out that she was so sorry... that she never meant to hurt Jack, never meant to hurt any of them... never wanted to hurt her own daughter. As Jack's parents closed in around her, moving her into the house, stroking Sara's heaving back and smoothing her frizzy brown hair amid all the boxes... they soothed her, saying they knew she didn't mean to hurt anyone.

Seeing their kindness... their gentleness... I began to cry.... 'This isn't about White, Sara...' they tried comforting '...It's about people....'

This isn't about White.... It's about people.... They said it three times. Honestly. Lovingly.

Sara, still weeping, nodded like she hadn't heard anything so true. She then lifted her head to their embrace and the clip ended.

I sniffed and wiped my eyes and quickly rang Char, but it went straight to voicemail.

Chapter Twenty-Eight

Light

It's not about White…. It's about people.

I couldn't get it out of my head all morning.

Char included the link on Jack's page too. In the three hours that it had been up, it collected over 400,000 views from her site alone. Comments were non-stop.

I tried one more time and finally got through.

'Where have you *been*?' Char exclaimed, her voice sounding raw.

'I'm sorry… I overslept.'

'Did you see the video?'

'I did. What happened?'

'The Fenners came to the house this morning and they only just left. They've been here for hours, talking to Mum the whole time—they talked to me too—we *all* talked, but yeah they only just left.'

'…*Why*…?' I couldn't quite understand. 'What prompted them to come?'

'They saw what I put up last night, that we were moving because Mum couldn't handle the backlash of the whole thing with Jack. Just before I came and met you, I had a row with her and posted it.'

'You *posted* that?' After everything that Teddy said to her last night. 'Why?' I found myself asking, wishing she would see the detriment of publicising every single thing that was going on in her life.

'Because she was going to cancel my account, because my site was going to be taken down,' she said flatly. 'Because she was going to obliterate the voice I thought people finally needed to hear and I wasn't sure whether there would be anything left when I got back from you guys.' I heard her sigh down the phone. 'And I was angry, that's why.'

'So now what?'

'Now… now I'm not.'

She didn't sound angry, I realised. In fact, she sounded determined. Resolute.

'And what about the move?'

'Not happening. Mum's going to talk to school, talk to the counselling people at her work. Make an effort to understand—' but she stopped short.

After a few seconds,

'Char…?'

'She's going to make an effort to understand why she thinks the way she does,' she finished her sentence, reiterating the very thing Teddy had encouraged *her* to do last night. 'She's going to go back to work and face her colleagues, face the consequences of her actions. Which I too need to do as well.'

'You?'

'C'mon Ivy,' she chided as if it were obvious. 'You

were there last night. You heard him. It's no different from what The Fenner's were saying this morning. Mum is *one* person, responsible only to sort *her* wrongs—not those of the entire world. And I'm not blameless here either,' she insisted, uncharacteristically. 'I've got things to sort out. But I think the video is a good start, don't you?'

'It's an amazing start,' I told her, knowing she probably didn't get her mother's permission to post it, or Jack's parents, but that neither were likely to object considering the message Char was trying to send out. Even without the words *THIS ISN'T ABOUT WHITE— IT'S ABOUT PEOPLE*, seeing Sara so ashamed, so vulnerable and human... there was absolutely nothing there in her that wasn't already present in everyone else to some degree.

After lunch, I kept hearing Mr and Mrs Fenner's voices in my head, and they were relentless while Mum and I walked to the cliff overlooking the place where Gran's ashes were to be scattered.

The shorter of the two men who wheeled Gran into the van was bolting her bench into a thick slab of concrete when we arrived, and the drone was out, with its white flag trailing, ready to dump its load.

'Everything's all set,' the man said finally, wiping the seat down with a cloth. 'Please, make yourselves comfortable.'

Mum and I went over to the bench and read the plaque:

THE ONLY WHITE THAT MATTERS IS THE LIGHT YOU BRING

'There is no rush,' the man assured. 'We're ready when you are.' He lifted his handset and motioned to the tall, slim figure on the headland below who was clearly controlling the drone out at sea.

Mum took a seat and stretched her arm out to me, wrapping it around my shoulder as I slid next to her. We sat for a few minutes, feeling the blazing sun, thinking of Gran.

'*The only white that matters is the light you bring,*' I said appreciatively after a few minutes, drowning out the Fenner's voices.

'Shall we do it?' Mum asked, to which I nodded, and a moment later, the drone, with its trailing white tail came up to eye level maybe a hundred meters out and dropped a little black cloud that disappeared almost instantly in the wind.

As I tried for the life of me to find a speck of her… a dark streak maybe, or a bright glint caught up in the air, I decided that white, *White*… didn't matter.

What mattered was what you left behind.

People.

The light you left with them.

Mum and I leaned our heads together when the ashes were gone.

Chapter Twenty-Nine

Ready

It seemed only fitting to do it in Gran's room, the place I had so naively thought I could outwake her from death.

The light was harsh this side of the house, direct, so I lowered the blind.

I set myself up on the little nest of sidetables in the middle of the empty room after Mum went back up for a few more hours rest. The phone kept falling over, catching my face in the shot, but I finally got the angle right with a wad of sticky tack the size of a golf ball.

I positioned my *Black 6* mortality mole perfectly in the middle of the screen, though I had to admit, the camera made it looked more like *Black 4.*

With my plaster nearby, I took in a deep breath, stared momentarily at the record button, and still certain, pressed it.

'I don't want to know when I'll die,' I said in a

clear, firm voice. 'Death has been on my mind every day since I was three years old, and before that, when I couldn't understand it, I was taught to look for it here.'

I put my finger to the dark spot, feeling already it wasn't a part of me.

'I don't want to look anymore,' I resolved. 'And the decision I'm making here… is for *me*, and me alone. It's what *I* want, how *I* want to be. No one is forcing me to do this. No one has pressured me to tint or hide—*this isn't my last resort*. In fact, I am confident that I will live well past my 50's at this rate, because I'm 16 years old, and *Black 6*.'

I focused on the dark spot, the digital one.

'Only I'm not actually *Black 6*. I… *am a human being*. A human being who doesn't want to look at every other human being with this as my filter anymore.'

I let the video carry on recording as I pressed my finger over the small lump, pushing it into my wrist, preparing myself.

'The hours that I've spent comparing myself to strangers… deciding whether or not they're worth talking to, spending time with… knowing they were doing the same to me on account of *this*… I've wasted *months*. And I've forgotten what it is to be human,' I said sadly. '*We've* forgotten what it is to be human.'

As I stared and wondered how a seemingly insignificant little mark could be responsible for so much, it occurred to me what it meant to be human, and what this little thing stuck to me was truly undermining.

'To me,' I said thoughtfully, 'being human is to show compassion. Empathy. And it's to be able to *accept* compassion and empathy… because it's our vulnerable, human side that allows us to finally connect with others.' My eyes narrowed on that edge, where black and white met. 'Yet how can we do any of that with this in the way? How can we connect with one another when this dictates who our friends will be... who we ought to love... and forces us to constantly see others—*or ourselves*—as not good enough? Not dark enough. And certainly never equal enough.'

Emboldened, I exhaled and hunched over my hand, ready. Without a blade or anything sharp, I simply poked underneath the edges of my dot with my fingernail. Gently round the edges I went, hoping for a sign of some give.

'I don't want to know when I will die,' I asserted, picking. 'My body can break beyond recognition, yet I cannot be injured to death like the insects and animals. We live in a world where death will come when it comes. I cannot force it.'

All of a sudden, a thin edge of the mole clearly lifted and I held my breath as the focus on the screen automatically blurred and sharpened for a moment.

Carefully, with almost no pressure at all, I slipped my nail underneath and worked around the full circumference of the beveled black, watching in amazement as its outer edges lifted from my pale skin like the tiny cap of a rotten, flat mushroom.

'I want to live in a world where death's place is at the end,' I determined, my voice quivering a little. 'Not at the beginning. Or throughout the middle. In those places, I just want to see light—*be* light. ...*Life*.'

Just then, I gasped slightly, for my finger slipped straight through the underside of the mole, slicing it completely free of my arm.

It sat there at the tip of my finger with its crusty

edge curled beneath my nail, and immediately I wanted it off me. Of course, when I looked at the spot it had come from, there was no blood, just as Teddy had said. Instead, there was a beautiful pale scar a pearly shade of white I never thought would be so welcome on my wrist.

'It's come off like a scab,' I said with wonder and giddying relief. '...A *scab*....'

Chapter Thirty

(one month)
Later

I sat on Gran's bench and held my face to the wind with my eyes closed. I knew she wasn't really there, but I could almost convince myself she was.

'You're famous,' a familiar voice startled me.

As I turned and looked, Teddy, gilded by weeks out in the orchards and fields, was hustling down a steep cut in the sandy chalk towards me.

'I thought I'd never see you again,' I gushed, standing up to meet him.

'Never see me?' He came round and hugged me without reservation, then smiled as if such a thing was unlikely. It was the same smile in fact that he had given me the last time I saw him, outside my gate. 'May I sit on your gran's bench?' he asked, accepting the invite as I sat and slid over, making more space for him.

'How did you know this is my gran's bench?'

'Because *my* gran brings me here,' he divulged

with great satisfaction.

He was in good spirits. I had never seen him this way. Of course, I had met him in his brother's week of white and realised I knew nothing outside of grief in him. And kindness.

'We come here every Sunday morning,' he added, making me feel closer to him somehow, for I had been coming at least three times a week. 'And she's told me all about your gran. Her best friend.'

'Did she now?'

Our conversation, as the sun touched the tip of the rocky little island out there, turned from old friendships to new family. He told me how his gran was making some progress with his father... how the family had allowed her a visit... and that his life felt full of change at the moment.'

'But of course, the biggest change is that wherever I look, I find more and more people without mortality moles,' he said, nudging me. 'You've changed the world Ivy.'

'And what makes you think *I* had anything to do with that?'

'C'mon....' He slid a foot away from me and looked dubiously at the plaque between us on Gran's bench. '*The only white that matters is the light you bring*,' he read. 'And the girl in the video... watched by over a billion people—a girl that has the same voice as you I hasten to add, said *I want to live in a world where death's place is at the end. Not at the beginning. Or throughout the middle. In those places, I just want to see light—be light. Life.*' He waited a beat, trying to crack me. '*Light*, Ivy,' he referred to the plaque again with a nod. 'Are you trying to tell me that *wasn't* you?'

'Maybe,' I said coyly, though I wasn't going to make any real effort to conceal my identity from him. 'So what if it was?'

Without a word he turned to the sea, closed the gap between us and stretched his legs out in front of him. I then watched as he comfortably curled his back against the varnished planks and closed his eyes with a satisfied smile.

'I'd like to think *I* had something to do with that video,' he pronounced contentedly, inhaling the sea breeze as he folded his hands onto his stomach.

'Yes, I think you might have,' I admitted, finding him beautiful there. Had it not been for him, I would never have felt the freedom I felt just then.

We were quiet for a long time after that.

The sea birds circled and settled on the rock in the distance just as the sun was setting and before it got too dark, I found myself telling Teddy of the world I imagined out there somewhere. A world where no one knew when they would die. A world where people met their end like the animals and insects we often envied. Maybe instead of having no idea of when death came, they'd stumble upon it with awe and wonder I told him, because the rest of their lives weren't full of fear.

'I mean, can you even *imagine* such a place—such an existence?' I asked under the rose quartz sky.

Teddy shook his head as though amazed at the thought.

'Almost, Ivy. *Almost....*'

ACKNOWLEDGEMENTS

I want to thank my husband Jon for filling the parental void my avid writing creates in the family home. His support and patience has been constant. I want to thank my children too for their understanding of the process. Their enthusiasm is constant. I want to thank John for the push in a different direction, Howard for helping me present the darker side of this story, Holly and Tim for their gracious honesty with it, and my friends… who kept asking when they could read it. (*You can now!*)

Of course, I want to thank the late Hugh Everett III, an American physicist who first proposed the many-worlds interpretation (MWI) of quantum physics, a concept from which this book has been inspired.

Shawn Terry Upton worked in children's education for twelve years before writing her first novel.

Originally from California, she met her husband while studying in London. They have three children and live in Somerset. *Death Dot* is her first published Young Adult Science Fiction novel.

For more information:

w w w . q u a n t a l o r e . c o m

Printed in Poland
by Amazon Fulfillment
Poland Sp. z o.o., Wrocław